Unwanted

Unwanted

Mary E. Sandford

AMBASSADOR INTERNATIONAL
GREENVILLE, SOUTH CAROLINA & BELFAST, NORTHERN IRELAND

www.ambassador-international.com

Unwanted

ISBN: 978-1-62020-998-1
eISBN: 978-1-62020-999-8
Library of Congress Control Number: 2019949182

This is a work of fiction. Names, characters, and incidents are all products of the author's imagination or are used for fictional purposes. Any resemblance to actual events or persons, living or dead, is entirely coincidental. Any mentioned brand names, places, and trademarks remain the property of their respective owners, bear no association with the author or the publisher, and are used for fictional purposes only.

Cover Design & Typesetting by Hannah Nichols
Ebook Conversion by Anna Riebe Raats

AMBASSADOR INTERNATIONAL
Emerald House
411 University Ridge, Suite B14
Greenville, SC 29601, USA
www.ambassador-international.com

AMBASSADOR BOOKS
The Mount
2 Woodstock Link
Belfast, BT6 8DD, Northern Ireland, UK
www.ambassadormedia.co.uk

The colophon is a trademark of Ambassador, a Christian publishing company.

For my brother Paul who rescued me from squash and bullies, "I'll see you soon."

CHAPTER ONE

UNHAPPY

I dashed to the washroom, a place with no privacy at all. Mary Ellen sat perched on the toilet closest to the door, feet dangling in midair. Her undies, that might have been pink once upon a time, hung around her ankles.

"Hi," Mary Ellen said. But she kept her eyes on her knees.

With a quiet, "mmm-huh," I took a seat at the other end of the row.

Even though Mary Ellen is way younger than me she knows this is not a time or place to chat. She didn't look at me. Which sure made me feel a lot better about such a humiliating situation.

The first time I'd walked into the washroom, I couldn't believe my eyes. Where were the stalls? And especially the doors for them. How could a washroom not have stalls like at school or a store? But, it didn't.

At The Home, four toilets sat in an embarrassing row across from four sinks with our little towels hanging above them. The towels that had to be folded and hung just right. Like a row of obedient children.

As if doing our private business in public wasn't bad enough, I also found out the windows had been painted so many times they were impossible to pry open. That's right, I tried. And I didn't believe for one minute that was an accident. They did it on purpose to keep us from escaping.

Unwanted

Ever since school started most of the girls hurried to the only washroom first thing. I got dressed before I went. To avoid the crowd. No one else seemed to care, but, to me, a washroom was not the place for so many girls at one time. All the splashing water and words going every which way were too much. At Gram's, we took turns. And we knocked.

A noise that I will not describe came from the other end of the row. I ignored it. No matter what, my favorite of all the girls here would always be Mary Ellen, which is why I cared about her future almost as much as mine. As far as I knew, she was the only five-year-old who'd ever been dumped at The Home. Everyone was supposed to be at least six. But, no one told any of us how she ended up here, going to first-grade when she was barely old enough to be in kindergarten.

Being as Mary Ellen was so little, it was no surprise Mrs. Petersen made her spend a lot of time right in that spot to make sure she didn't have another accident. Like the one she had on the way to church her first Sunday. That was way back when Mary Ellen got here two months after me which meant we were kind of new together.

But that wasn't the only reason I liked Mary Ellen more than any of the other girls. I liked her for lots of reasons. Like how everyone says we look alike since we both have blue eyes with our dark hair, and, after her first Saturday, we had matching haircuts, too. And, because we like the same things, the color blue and meatloaf with mashed potatoes. Plus, Mary Ellen is plucky, which I admire, and that's why I pretend we're sisters. But I can never tell anyone that.

I finished and headed to the sink closest to the window. Glancing in the mirror, I saw Mary Ellen hop off her throne and pull herself together. I turned on the water at the sink next to mine.

"Thanks, Debbie," Mary Ellen said. She rinsed her hands and wiped them down her dress, instead of using her towel. When she copied me like that, I knew she was a smart little cookie.

"This is my favorite dress," she said spinning to make the skirt flare out.

I smiled. "It's a very pretty shade of blue." But, a pinch of sadness pulled the smile right off my face. I could tell Mary Ellen knew how awful it felt to get stuck with an ugly dress for a whole week. Doing my best to sound happy, I added, "It's almost the same color as mine."

Mary Ellen spun again.

"Do you think it will snow today?" She stopped her spin and watched her skirt slow down to a swish.

"Sometimes it snows a lot in December."

"I love snow," Mary Ellen said. She lifted her chin a bit like she'd figured out how to hate it here and still love some things.

"I do, too." Another connection. "Especially fresh snow."

"It's the best." Mary Ellen wrapped her arms around my waist and squeezed. We were the last ones in the washroom, so I hugged her back.

"But I can't be late." Mary Ellen dashed out the door.

I squeezed a dab of toothpaste onto my toothbrush. Humming, I brushed and sang the jingle in my head, "You'll wonder where the yellow went, when you brush your teeth with Pepsodent."

After I rinsed my mouth, I examined my teeth in the mirror. They were white, but were they whiter? I sang the jingle again, "You'll wonder where the yellow went when you brush your teeth with Pepsodent." It wasn't much of a song, but I liked to sing so I sang once more holding my toothbrush like a microphone.

Unwanted

In the Big Girls' Room, I put on my coat and got my books. The dormitory was empty, so I scrambled down the stairs and out the girl's side door. I didn't button my coat. The cold doesn't bother me; besides, I loved the dress I had for this week. There were four pretty buttons going down the front to the waist, the kind where the thread didn't show. The bodice was dark blue, and both the Peter Pan collar and the skirt were a lighter blue with tiny dark blue polka dots. Out of the three dresses in my size, this one was the prettiest.

I hurried down the cracked narrow sidewalk alongside The Home. Straight ahead across the street, Roberta's dad sat in the driver's seat of his shiny new 1958 Buick Riviera with the motor running. Just like every other morning, Mr. Solomon read the *Chicago Tribune* while he waited to give Roberta a ride to school, which seemed plain silly to me. Anyone should be able to walk two-and-a-half blocks. Roberta pranced down their flagstone steps in her black patent-leather Mary Janes. Her little sister and her mother followed close behind. Mr. Solomon peered over the top edge of his newspaper with a smile anyone could see was prideful.

"Mother, look, there's that girl from my class. The one who lives in The Home." Roberta used a loud, nasty voice, like she wanted me to hear. And, she always acted like she didn't know my name. Like I wasn't good enough to even have one. She pointed, too, as if her mother was actually paying attention, which she wasn't. Her mother was too busy carefully closing their fancy front door. Not one house on the whole block had a door like it. The entire top half had giant stained-glass flowers. Red and blue. It looked gaudy if you asked me.

"Just look at her," Roberta said as loud as ever. "Do you see the dreadful dress she's wearing?"

I stopped staring and yanked my coat closed. Holding my books over my chest, I ran pell-mell like Bambi's father toward school.

But I still heard Roberta shouting, "It looks like she borrowed it from her four-year-old sister."

Around the corner, I slowed down. Gram always told me I should love my enemies, but Roberta was so mean it seemed impossible. She knew full well I didn't have a sister. And that hurt more than her not liking my dress.

If only I hadn't dawdled getting ready for school, I would have been long gone when Roberta came out of her perfect house. Even if Roberta did have a mother and a father and her own little sister, it didn't matter to me. Not one bit. I knew someday I would have a family again. And a little sister. For sure, my new family would be way better than Roberta's.

CHAPTER TWO

UNFAIR

Roberta stood at our classroom door like she thought she was a policeman. I opened my history book, so I wouldn't have to look at her. My mind wandered back to the first day of school when our teacher Mr. Kelly had said, "Every Monday afternoon throughout seventh grade we will be enjoying filmstrips. Their content will show us the exciting history not included in our books."

It turned out our books were too old to teach us anything about World War II, which was fine by me. While that first filmstrip was running, and I was trying not to think about any of it, Mr. Kelly had told us the way the German soldiers were marching was called goose-stepping. I'd laughed right out loud, even though laughing always got me in a lot of trouble. I knew it wasn't funny, but what happened to my family because of the war was a done deal. Laughing at the war was way better than crying and having everyone feel sorry for me any day.

Lucky for me, Mr. Kelly really loves films; so, on our first day, he gave me a frown and went on explaining. I tried to like Mr. Kelly, but I knew he'd hated me first thing that morning. He'd sat at his big oak desk in the front of the classroom and read out each student's name. Most of the students called out "here" like a person ought to, but, when he read Roberta Solomon's name, she said, "I'm here, and I'm just tickled pink."

Mr. Kelly had stopped and looked up with a smile showing off dimples that made almost everyone in the room like him immediately. It wasn't my fault Spencer came right after Solomon; so, after Roberta made such a fuss, my "here" sounded almost rude. Mr. Kelly had his mind made up right then and there about me. With that first awkward word I'd said to him and the laughing that first day, whenever he looked my way, his mouth was ruler straight.

Since today was Monday, at two o'clock sharp Mr. Kelly had left the room to get the film projector putting Roberta in charge like he did every time he had to leave our room. She was the teacher's pet, and I was the opposite.

When Mr. Kelly pushed the projector cart into the room, Roberta glared at me. I guess she was mad she couldn't tattle today. Of course, Mr. Kelly didn't notice. He was too busy unbuttoning his brown suit jacket which he did a hundred times a day. In my opinion he just wanted to show off his matching vest. He wore that same suit and vest every day with a crisp white shirt and one of his three ties.

Mr. Kelly fiddled and fussed making a production of getting everything set up, especially getting the cart to an exact spot behind all the desks between rows three and four. I held my breath until he turned on the projector light.

The beam of light made a path up the aisle filled with dancing glitter. I knew it was only dust in the air, but I loved it anyway. Until Mr. Kelly stepped around the cart and blocked my view of it. Like always. I suppose he wasn't doing it on purpose, but it felt like he was.

He finally flipped the switch to start the reels rolling. My best friend at school, Doris, sitting in the third row third seat, wiggled her eyebrows at me before she turned to watch the film. The loud hum of the clickety-ticking projector filled up the room.

How could I bear another WWII film? Our class already had to watch more than I'd ever want to count. I squeezed my eyes shut as tight as a new pair of saddle shoes, which of course I'd never have now. Mr. Kelly cleared his throat. Loudly. I peeked between my eyelashes. His glaring face zeroed in on me. Rubbing my eyes, I stared right past him to the screen he'd set up in front of the blackboard.

Paying attention to the filmstrip was out of the question; instead, I closed my left eye and then my right. Interesting. With my left eye closed, I could see the back of the five heads in front of me, each one leaning a bit one way or the other. With my right eye closed, row after row of German soldiers marched across the screen up front. *They were supposed to look scary.* But, if you asked me, I'd say they looked down-right silly with their arms and legs going straight up and down. It's no wonder they lost the war marching like that.

What was wrong with me, thinking such mean things? Gram had always told me to be careful with my thinking because sometimes I let it run away from me. But I cannot think about Gram here, and, even though the mean sound of Roberta's voice before school still echoed in my head, I knew that was the worst place my thoughts could run off to now.

Instead, I focused on fixing my loose bobby pin. Opening it with my teeth, I slid it back into place to hold my growing bangs to the side. But still, my heart hurt like someone was twisting it right out of my chest.

My eyes wandered across the room to Roberta in the first seat of the first row. I couldn't stop them. She slipped her hand under her long honey-colored hair and let it fall like silk down to her waist. Perfect as usual. If only us girls at The Home didn't have to keep our hair short, I could have hair exactly like Roberta's. Not the same color, but even dark brown hair could look perfect, long, and swishy.

I checked the clock above the screen. Ten to three. Only ten minutes and I'd get to my favorite part of the day. The only time I had when no one was in charge of me.

The skinny black second hand made its way around the face of the clock jerking past each dot between the numbers. Sort of the same jerky way the German soldiers marched.

I pressed my lips tight against my teeth to keep from laughing. It seemed impossible to stop thinking about goose-stepping, what with the projector lollygagging at the back of the room near my desk. And the second hand marching around the clock. Why couldn't it just sweep along smoothly like the one on Daddy's watch used to?

The projector stopped abruptly with a blast of light hitting the screen and the sound of the end of the film flapping around and around covering up the sighs all over the room. Reaching into my desk, I got out the books I needed for homework, Arithmetic, Social Studies, and my black and white composition book. I opened it. Mostly mine was filled with page after page of sentences I'd had to write for punishment. On page one I'd had to write, "I will not daydream in class." I'd had to write that one more times than I'd want to count. But, not today.

I forced myself to keep my eyes off the clock. And Doris. I'd laugh for sure if she saw me holding back a laugh because she'd make googly eyes at me, and I'd be laughing out loud while Doris kept hers inside, and then I'd be the one who had to write, "I will not laugh in an unladylike manner and cause a disturbance in class." One hundred times. And I already knew that would take longer than all my other homework put together.

Doris was the only good thing about being stuck in Mr. Kelly's room all day. Even if I didn't get one of the other seventh-grade teachers who might have liked kids from The Home, I could still endure Mr. Kelly with Doris in the same class.

Now, I kept my eyes off the clock and Mr. Kelly. Still, without even a glimpse at the second hand, I knew exactly how it marched past all the numbers. A laugh started to escape my lips. I coughed to cover it up making sure I put my hand over my mouth like a lady ought to. And also, to stay out of trouble. I would not give Mr. Kelly any reason to take away my time today.

Then I heard him. "Deborah Spencer."

CHAPTER THREE

UNJUST

"Yes, Mr. Kelly." I stood like a soldier in the aisle between the fifth and sixth row.

Mr. Kelly did not look at me when he said, "Be seated and remain at your desk when the class is dismissed."

I sat, but on the inside my heart and my soul were still standing. My hope for a few minutes to myself vanished.

Concentrating on folding my hands on top of the books I'd stacked, I could still see the rest of the class. All the other students sat on the edge of their seats with their books clutched to their chests or held with an old-fashioned strap. Except for Roberta. She balanced her brand-spanking new leather valise on her knees.

The second hand clicked to twelve and the minute hand followed. Three o'clock. I clenched my teeth.

"Class dismissed." Mr. Kelly's voice sounded nothing like the one he used for me.

Thirty-four pairs of feet scrambled down the aisles and lined up across the front of the room. Mr. Kelly carefully turned the glass door knob and pulled open the door. As my classmates filed out, he made eye contact with each student and smiled. When Roberta passed by, his smile got bigger. Then Jacob Weinberg, who was new last week,

dropped his arithmetic book. When he went to pick it up, he acciden-
tally kicked it out the door.

Doris turned around as quick as a scared mouse and mouthed, "I'll
wait for you."

"Careful there, buddy," Mr. Kelly said to Jacob, his dimples almost
exploding. With an ever so friendly nod at the last student in line, he
pushed the door closed. He took plenty of time turning around. By
then both his friendliness and his dimples had evaporated.

Mr. Kelly picked up the black felt eraser from the wood ledge
along the bottom of the blackboard. Moving as slow as a turtle, he
erased Monday, December 1, 1958. He made a sharp left turn with the
eraser when he got to: Your full name, Mr. Kelly, Room 209, making
a straight path under the heading we had to put on all our papers. It
seemed to me like he might as well erase that, too. Everyone ought
to know it by now, but he slowly slid past it and erased all the rest of
his precise penmanship.

The second hand kept goose-stepping around the face of the clock.
It didn't seem funny at all anymore because the clock read almost ten
minutes after three. If only I knew why I was being kept after.

Ignoring Mr. Kelly's intentional dilly-dallying, I made up an arithmetic story problem in my head. The Home was two-and-a-half blocks
from school. After school I had to get all the way upstairs, and say,
"Good afternoon," to Mrs. Petersen no later than three-thirty. If I hurried, I could get there in less than ten minutes, would I have time to
talk to Doris if I left by three-fifteen? The correct answer should be
yes, but with Mr. Kelly being part of the equation I could only hope.

Finally, Mr. Kelly placed the eraser back on its dusty shelf, brushed
his hands together, and at long last turned around. Without looking at

me, he picked up a single sheet of paper off his desk. With a frown on his face, he walked slower than a snail to my desk, last seat, sixth row.

I sat perfectly still, which always seemed harder for me than it should be.

"It seems you are completely incapable of sitting still, Miss Spencer, no matter what the circumstances." Mr. Kelly glared at me.

My mouth dropped open.

Before I could protest, Mr. Kelly pointed his finger at my scuffed brown oxfords. "You are tapping your feet. In fact, you have been tapping your feet ever since I closed the door. You need to learn how to be still."

"Sorry."

"Sorry doesn't change anything. You must learn to contain yourself." Mr. Kelly didn't have to add, "all you kids from The Home are such a problem." I knew he was thinking it. He stood perfectly still like he was trying to show off his perfect stillness.

I'd never figure out what made being still so gall-darn important anyway. I couldn't see the use of it. Still, I prayed there wouldn't be a next time. But, with over three weeks of school before Christmas vacation and more than six months before I finally got out of Mr. Kelly's class, I wouldn't even bet on it myself.

Mr. Kelly cleared his throat slower than I thought anyone could, before he said, "Do you recall your Arithmetic homework?"

"Yeah. I mean, yes sir." I was sure I'd written out the steps of each story problem in complete sentences. Every answer was about the same as Doris' when we compared them before we lined up this morning. But, the third seat third row was glaringly empty. I had no idea what Mr. Kelly was getting at.

Mr. Kelly smiled one of his you-are-really-in-trouble-now smiles which he saved for me and did not include dimples.

"Explain to me why you put this little star over the 'i' you wrote when you chose to write Debbie instead of your full given name?"

"Okay. Sir. It is. I'm so glad you could tell, it was a star. I mean, I made it so tiny I wasn't sure anyone else could even see it." With a glance at the clock, almost three twenty, I rushed on.

"You see, I know you really like Roberta, and I know she's been putting Bobbie with a little heart over the 'i' on her papers for over a week."

At this, Mr. Kelly's face turned red and he opened his mouth. That's when his annoying slowness tripped him up because I didn't wait to hear what he might say. I kept right on talking.

"But I haven't been cheating off her papers or anything like that. Roberta, or should I say, Bobbie, has been bragging about it at recess every day, so I know you let her change the way she wrote her name even though you told us at the beginning of the year that we always, always have to put our proper name and your name and our room number, 209, on the top of every paper. But now, since you let Roberta, Bobbie, add that heart I just knew it would be fine for me to try something like that, too. Isn't it, Mr. Kelly?"

Mr. Kelly unpursed his lips long enough to say, "You are dismissed." He spun around and marched to the blackboard where he began to write Tuesday. Before he got to the December 2, 1958, part, I had my hand on the glass door knob. Silently, I prayed, *Thank you Jesus,* and it wasn't a swear. I meant it.

But Mr. Kelly was not one to lose easily, at least, not without getting the last word. As I stepped into the hall, he called out, "Debbie should be spelled with a 'y'."

CHAPTER FOUR

UNCERTAIN

Outside, Doris was long gone. A few girls were walking way down the block on Spaulding, but none of them had on Doris' navy-blue coat with the sailor collar hanging down in the back. She loved that coat because her father had been in the Navy before he came home from the war.

Doris didn't have the kind of fancy clothes Roberta wore, but hers were way better than any of the things I had to wear. She also had the best hair. A golden-brown pageboy down to her shoulders with bangs. I would die for bangs. But, Miss Ritz, the headmistress at The Home said, "Bangs need trimming far too often."

I wasn't at all surprised Doris wasn't waiting, because I knew she always had to get home to finish her long list of chores before supper. I never saw Doris outside of school, which was sort of odd since we were such chums. But her dad was really strict and didn't let Doris have friends over. And, of course, at The Home no one ever got to go anywhere besides school and church. And none of the kids would dream of inviting anyone over. Even if we could.

Thinking about Doris was slowing me down which meant I had to really rush now. Waiting until tomorrow to tell her how I stood up to Mr. Kelly was all right with me. As soon as Noreen and Sharon got back to The Home from high school, I could tell them. Not that Noreen would approve in any way, but Sharon would love to hear every little part. And, she'd laugh in all the right places.

Sharon was newer to The Home than me. She had crazy curly auburn hair, so Miss Ritz made her keep it in a ponytail. Probably because anyone could tell cutting it short would only make it crazier. Right away I knew, the day Sharon brought her stuff into the Big Girls' Room that Noreen wanted Sharon to be her best friend, which didn't make any sense to me. They were nothing alike.

Sharon acted a lot like her hair. She loved using silly words like *okey-doke* and *peachy-keen*. Noreen on the other hand was extremely quiet and hardly ever laughed. Nothing against Noreen, but I could tell Sharon already thought I was more fun. She always said, "I know I'm a flibbertigibbet. I live for fun."

What a crazy thing to say. But it was way more interesting than sitting on her bed reading or praying with her rosary like Noreen.

Stepping into the street, I walked along the curb to avoid the sidewalk in front of the Sun View apartment buildings. They never shoveled. Too bad I didn't wear boots. It was only because the pair that fit over my size eight-and-a-half oxfords were boy's galoshes with two broken buckles. I couldn't stand wearing them in public. Even though walking over icy smashed-down snow without boots slowed me down a lot.

Besides that, since it had snowed two days ago, I was stuck with the worst coat for the whole winter. It's made of itchy brown wool, my least favorite color, and there's no trim at all or nice buttons. The buttons were made of the same ugly material as the coat and always got caught in the raggedy holes.

My throat tightened up thinking of my coat. I blamed the ugly old thing for what Roberta said this morning. She was probably planning to call my coat ugly when she noticed which dress I had on, and I know she heard Doris tell me how pretty it is the last time I wore it. I didn't care if Roberta didn't like my dress, but she didn't have to remind me about not having a little sister. Or a family.

A green and yellow Checker cab zipped around the corner. The cabbie laid on his horn interrupting my thoughts. I hopped back to the sidewalk.

Keeping my eyes on every step, I knew what Gram would say about Roberta. "Love your neighbor as yourself." Plus, she'd tell me that didn't just mean Doris and Noreen and Sharon. It meant Roberta, too. I also knew Gram was right, but, as far as I could see, no kid could ever think anything good about Roberta.

Turning the corner onto Evergreen, I ran the rest of the way. The Home, red brick with tall white pillars on each side of the double front doors, loomed up into the clear cold sky. No other place in the whole neighborhood took up at least five lots and had a fence across the front and a play yard on the side. I wondered why everyone called it The Home. Nothing about it made me think home.

Reaching the black cast-iron gate in front, I unlatched it, swung it open, and stepped through. Forcing out a two-note laugh, "Ha-ha," I closed it as quietly as I could and added, "You're not clanging shut today."

With that, I took the concrete steps two at a time, trying not to recall the sound of the gate clanging shut the first day I'd laid eyes on it.

Uncle Lloyd had held it open for me. "You know your mother can't take care of you," he'd said.

I hated him for saying that. Like it didn't bother him at all. Besides, I was sure I could take care of myself. Any twelve-year-old could. Mostly. Just because he never had to take care of himself, with Gram always doing everything for him, didn't mean I couldn't manage.

Uncle Lloyd swung the gate open wider. "Don't make this any harder than it has to be."

Crossing my arms over my chest, I had lifted my eyebrows with my meanest look. I wasn't moving until he explained where he was taking me and why.

Uncle Lloyd grabbed my arm and pulled me along. "It's not her fault, Debbie. It's because of your dad."

Another hateful thing to say.

Then letting the gate slam shut he added the meanest words of all. "And because your Gram died."

Now, every time I went through the gate, if it clanged shut, that awful sound rang in my ears along with Uncle Lloyd's words.

CHAPTER FIVE

UNSPOKEN

I looked through the plain glass of the heavy front doors. The coast was clear. Turning the big brass knob, I opened it slowly, but it slipped out of my grip, and the door hit the wall with a bang. Maybe Miss Ritz would be busy.

No such luck.

As I passed the office, the headmistress looked up. "Good afternoon, Debbie. Please don't bang the door."

"Sorry," I said over my shoulder. Hustling, I climbed the wide wooden staircase. "And good afternoon, Miss Ritz," I added, but I don't think she heard me.

That was odd. Why didn't Miss Ritz say anything about me using the front door? We were supposed to use the girls' door which was halfway down the side of the building. But it always got stuck when I tried to open it fast, and the knob had to be jiggled just right, which took forever. Besides, I ended up using the same stairs to get to the second floor anyway, so coming in the front door saved a lot of time.

Today, I was glad I didn't get in trouble because I didn't have time for it. I turned right at the top of the stairs, and almost dropped my books trying to get the dormitory door open quickly. Swinging it open, I spotted Mrs. Petersen tuning her radio in her private bedroom at the front of the long room with twenty beds lined up, ten along each side.

"Good afternoon, Mrs. Petersen."

She turned and smoothed the old-fashioned white apron tied around her ample middle. I suppose she wore it to protect her pink house dress. But I wasn't sure why or from what, I just prayed she wouldn't pick up the watch hanging around her neck and nestled on what could only be called a bosom. I gave the housemother the best smile I could manage in a hurry.

"Good afternoon, Debbie." Mrs. Petersen fumbled with her watch. She held it near the end of her nose, peering over wire rimmed glasses to check the time.

I hurried down the center aisle ignoring all the girls. Some of them were sitting on the edge of their beds reading. Others knelt on the floor using a bed to do homework. And a few sat on their beds face-to-face with another girl, their knees almost touching as they clapped hands with each other.

Mrs. Petersen followed me. "Humph, you barely made it here in time," she said, using her I-am-very-stern voice. "What took you so long?"

I turned around to her. "I'm really sorry." Shifting my books into one arm, I looked at them instead of Mrs. Petersen. "I was walking with my school friend Doris. I guess the talking slowed me down."

"Very well, Debbie, but you know I cannot ignore tardiness."

"Yes, Mrs. Petersen."

Bustling along to the other end of the dorm, I felt my face get red. I hated lying, especially to Mrs. Petersen. She wasn't anything like a real mother, not someone you could talk to about important things and all. That didn't surprise me, because as far as I could tell, adults never cared about kids' feelings.

Still, everyone knew our housemother had the heart of a teddy bear despite always trying to be strict. Sometimes, if a girl was lucky, she might even get a hug. And then she'd really appreciate that marshmallow bosom.

In this case, the lie couldn't be helped. Mrs. Petersen always followed the rules. If I told her I'd been kept after school, it wouldn't matter if I hadn't done anything wrong, or that Mr. Kelly had let me go without any punishment sentences or anything. She'd still probably make me clean the washroom again. Or maybe scrub the stairs, which took much longer since there were nineteen of them. But even worse than any cleaning could possibly be, she'd surely make me have lights out early. Which wasn't at all fair to Noreen and Sharon, being as there was only one overhead light in the Big Girls' Room.

I flipped it on as soon as I got to the room.

All four of the beds had chenille spreads. Yellow. Green. Pink. And blue. They were nowhere near new, but still much better than the gray wool blankets on every bed in the dormitory. With a bedspread no one could tell if you'd folded the white sheet over the top edge of your blanket, which seemed so unnecessary. I dropped my books on the faded blue chenille one, which reminded me why I had that bed.

Lucky for me, a month after I got dumped at The Home, I'd been moved into the small bedroom at the end of the dormitory closest to the alley. Everyone called it the Big Girls' Room. Usually only high school girls stayed there, but both Linda and Patricia had graduated high school in June and moved out of The Home a few weeks later.

Then in August, Kathleen went to live with an aunt in Texas, leaving only Noreen in the Big Girls' Room. Two days later, Miss Ritz had decided since I was the oldest girl in the dormitory, I should move so Noreen wouldn't be alone.

I was glad to get out of the noisy dormitory which sometimes smelled awful. Especially when we had baked beans for supper, or, on Fridays, the day before the laundry was done. Turned out Noreen didn't mind being alone. She hardly ever talked, but at least we got to keep our light on until eight o'clock instead of seven-thirty like the dormitory.

When Sharon got to The Home on Labor Day right before school started, I made myself scarce. Thankfully they didn't make me move out. The first minute we were alone in the Big Girls' Room I found out Sharon wasn't a girl for secrets.

"So, what are you two in for," she said like we were all in jail.

It did feel like that sometimes.

Noreen blinked at her. "Well—" she started and then stopped. Her eyes got red and she blinked again, faster.

The answer flashed through my head. Noreen and Paul Sheehan were Irish twins, born in the same year, but not on the same day, who got to The Home over a year before I did. At The Home, girls and boys were always kept apart, which was a shame for Noreen and Paul because practically the only time they saw each other was at meals, and, even then, they weren't allowed to sit together. Boys and girls each had their own side in the dining hall separated by a wide aisle where the workers rushed back and forth from the kitchen bringing bowls of food to the square tables.

One night, a week after I was in the Big Girls' Room, Noreen had started talking after the light was out. She told me they were Catholic, and that she was still planning on being a nun, and how she kept her rosary hidden in her drawer inside a sock along with the little statue of the Pope her brother had won for reciting all his prayers by heart in fifth grade. The statue was porcelain and had a gold cross painted on its chest that Noreen said was real gold, but it didn't seem possible to me. Whoever heard of real gold paint? But Noreen wasn't one for lying, so it must be true.

"Since we're cell mates," Sharon said, her words shattering the awkward silence, "I thought we should get the history out of the way." She looked from Noreen to me.

I couldn't think of what to say. Probably most of the girls here assumed I was an orphan like them. I couldn't tell anyone about my mother. I couldn't even think about it. Noreen probably didn't know she came to my rescue, but she did.

"My mom and—" Noreen stopped and took a breath—"Paul, my brother and I came . . . last year. Our parents were in a car crash three days after Thanksgiving."

"I never knew that," I said. I'd felt pretty sorry for myself when Thanksgiving had been such a non-holiday here, but it must have been really hard for Noreen and Paul.

Sharon nodded like she knew all about a parent dying.

I didn't know Noreen's whole story because I'd never cared enough to ask. My face burned with shame at what Gram would have said if she knew how selfish I'd been. I yanked open my drawer to keep them from seeing my embarrassment.

"A drunk driver hit them," Noreen said. "It was only three in the afternoon on a Sunday."

My heart beat so fast I thought it would bust right out of my chest. No one should be drunk at three in the afternoon. On a Sunday. Especially not a mother. But I couldn't think about that. I concentrated on moving my things to the drawer below mine.

"That's awful," Sharon said. "My father disappeared when I was a baby. My mom had . . . tuberculosis."

"I'm so-sorry," Noreen said, putting her arm around Sharon.

I mumbled my *sorry* and closed my new drawer, leaving the old one open. "Um, you can have this one."

"Thanks." Sharon took the box she'd brought off her bed and turned it upside down over the open drawer. Socks, a hairbrush, and underwear tumbled out landing in a heap with a thud. Sharon pushed it shut. "So, what was it Mrs. Peter–men called this room?"

"Petersen," Noreen said. "Everyone calls this the Big Girls' Room. I think the best part is our door. It's probably so our light won't keep the other girls awake because we get to stay up later. I like the privacy most of all."

"And, it smells better," I said trying to make things light.

Sharon laughed. Then she opened her mouth as if to ask me something. The sound of Mrs. Petersen's ringing bell interrupted us.

"Suppertime," Mrs. Petersen called.

"Peachy-keen," Sharon said. "I'm absolutely starved. I could eat a horse, don't ya know."

I laughed louder than I should have.

"I'll show you the way," Noreen said.

Following behind them that day, I remember Noreen explaining how we all had assigned seats and the no-talking rule. I remember following them and trying to stop thinking about my mother. Wishing I never thought of her. Wishing I still had a family so much my stomach hurt. And worse, wishing I could figure out a way to have a different mother.

A better one.

CHAPTER SIX

UNFORTUNATE

Now, it was only a quarter to four so Sharon and Noreen weren't back from school yet. I left my books on my bed and went to the washroom. Mary Ellen sat perched in her usual spot.

We both got off the commode at the same time. Mary Ellen giggled and rushed to a sink to turn on the water for me.

"Thank you," I said showing her how to be polite.

"Look, what I got today." Mary Ellen pointed at her forehead where a blue star was stuck smack-dab in the middle.

"Good for you."

"I got in line very quietly all day. Mrs. Petersen said she's proud of me."

"I'm sure she is," I said. "I'm proud of you, too." I hoped she knew I cared for her way more than Mrs. Petersen ever could.

"Thanks."

Opening the door to leave, I gave Mary Ellen a special little sister pat on top of her head.

"Is Mrs. Petersen looking?"

I checked the dormitory. Her bedroom door was open, but she was nowhere in sight. "Nope, all's clear."

"She must of forgot me," Mary Ellen said with a grin.

I held the door open and told her, "today must be your lucky day." Mary Ellen skipped to her bed, which was really only half of one skip. Her bed was the last one in the row at this end of the dormitory. The door to the washroom and the door to the Big Girls' Room are side by side, which means our door is right next to her bed. She picked up a *Little Golden Book* with a picture of a white puppy sniffing a green lizard on the cover and held it up for me to see.

"Looks like a good book," I said. Someone had closed the door to the Big Girls' Room. "Maybe, I can read it to you later."

Reaching for the doorknob, I heard Sharon's voice, "I'm so, so, so, sorry, Noreen, but maybe they were wrong."

Pulling the door open quickly, I got inside. Noreen's sobs were muffled with her face in her pillow, but loud enough to make me shut the door fast. If Mrs. Petersen heard the sobs, things were bound to get way too complicated for all of us.

Sharon leaned over Noreen, who was curled up on her bed. "Maybe they were wrong," Sharon said again patting her back.

"Wrong about what?"

"On the way home from school we walked by some boys on the corner," Sharon said. "One of them had a transistor radio. He was telling the others about a school . . . on fire."

I reached over and smoothed Noreen's hair back. Dishwater blonde, her hair was so thin her scalp showed through. Seeing her scalp somehow made her sobs seem way worse, and it made me think being a nun wasn't such a bad idea for Noreen since then no one would ever see her hair.

"What school?" I whispered.

"He said, 'Our Lady of the Angels'." Sharon's words were so quiet, I had to read her lips. "We don't know for sure," she added in a regular voice.

Noreen pulled her face out of her pillow. Her eyes were so red it looked like she'd been crying for a month. She gulped in air. "But we heard him," she said and flung herself back to her pillow.

"But, that's the school . . ." I let my voice trail off. I didn't want to say the school Noreen and Paul used to go to. I couldn't say that. Not if their old school was maybe . . . burning down.

Noreen kept sobbing while Sharon patted her back. I gently tried to get her hair to lay right. How awful could I be letting my thoughts run away from me about Noreen's hair at a time like this?

Sharon mouthed, "I don't know what to do."

I knew immediately what Gram would say, "Let's pray about it."

But Noreen probably wouldn't like the way Gram taught me to pray, just talking to God instead of using a rosary. I wanted to make her feel better. But, how?

Mrs. Petersen would surely give out one of her hugs for something like this, but a hug didn't seem like enough for Noreen now. Maybe the boy with the transistor had been wrong. I needed to know the truth, so Noreen could stop crying and go back to her rosary and praying.

"I'm going to find out what really happened," I mouthed to Sharon.

"How?" she mouthed back.

That was definitely a problem, but it didn't stop me from adding, "I'll be right back," and heading out the door. Rushing through the dormitory I was glad the girls were busy and noisy, so maybe no one would hear Noreen before I got back.

Mrs. Petersen had the little black radio perched on the nightstand right next to the rocking chair she sat in all the time, but I'd never heard her listening to the news. All that ever came out of her radio was classical music. Besides, she would turn this into a big event, and I was hoping it wouldn't come to that. I had to find another way.

Slowing down at the first bed, I peeked into Mrs. Petersen's room. She leaned over her bed smoothing her pink, not faded, chenille bedspread around a plump pillow while violin music filled the air. I slipped past, opened the door to the stairs, and turned to close it as quickly and quietly as I could.

"What are you up to?"

CHAPTER SEVEN

UNBEARABLE

I gasped. "You startled me."

Paul, Noreen's brother, leaned against the railing behind me grinning. Everyone called him a dreamboat, and I guess he was for an older boy. His happy-go-lucky face made it clear he hadn't heard a thing about any fire at his old school. I knew he wouldn't break into sobs like Noreen, but he'd surely be upset once I told him why I was tiptoeing around.

"Noreen is . . . " I hesitated. Paul's face changed in an instant to alarm and something else. Maybe the face of a protector.

"Upset," I added finding a word that might ease him into the facts.

"Why," Paul demanded. "What happened? Where is she?" He reached for the door to the girl's dormitory.

"No. Don't." I blocked the door. "Maybe you can help."

Paul stopped but did not move away.

"You see, on the way home from school, Sharon and Noreen overheard some . . . news."

"What news?"

"I guess some school is on fire," I said trying to sound calm. "They heard or at least they think they heard that it's at—" my throat tightened up. I hated to go on, but, somehow, I forced the words out. "Your old school Our Lady of the Angels."

I hurried on as fast as I could before Paul did anything that would get him in trouble. "I was just going to find out if there really is a fire and if it's really your school. Mrs. Petersen isn't the right person to ask so I'm not sure how to find out. I need to get back as soon as I can before Noreen . . . " I let my voice trail off, but Paul didn't seem to notice.

"I saw Miss Ritz leave," he said like he was thinking out loud. "I couldn't figure out why she would leave early like that. I don't think she left for the day. She had her coat on and that long green scarf she puts on her head and wraps around her neck. But she didn't have that big black satchel she always carries. I can't figure it out. She never leaves her satchel here overnight."

I let out my breath surprised I'd been holding it. I'd thought for sure Miss Ritz would know what's going on.

"And I saw her lock up her office." Paul looked over the railing.

I did, too. At the end of the girls' staircase, Miss Ritz's office was dark. Next to her office was the front door and then the boys' stairs. I always thought it was strange that the boys and girls had separate stairs. What was the use of that seeing as how the landing at the top connected them anyway? *Focus,* I yelled at myself. *And stop letting your thoughts run off!*

No one was supposed to use the front door except for visitors. Maybe I got away with it earlier because Miss Ritz already knew about a school on fire and wasn't really paying attention.

Paul's eyes traveled the short distance from the office door to the front door. I could almost see the wheels in his head spinning. Lucky for him I'm a quick thinker. "If you get in trouble for leaving, Noreen will be more upset," I said. "Besides, I don't see how leaving would help us find out anything anyway."

Paul pounded his fist on the railing scowling.

"Wait," I blurted out. "I know where there's a radio, and, if we're careful, no one will know we turned it on."

"Where?"

"In the infirmary. And, right now, it's probably empty because I know none of the girls are in there."

"None of the boys either." Paul hustled down the stairs and cut through the front parlor past the black and white television. For a second, I wondered if we should try to find the news on that. No. When it was turned on once a week on Sunday nights for Lassie, everyone could hear it loud and clear as soon as someone opened the dormitory door.

Paul was halfway down the back hall making me hurry to catch up. The door to the infirmary stood open. He stopped and stepped aside to let me in first closing the door quietly behind us.

Four white beds with white bedding stood in a silent row. "See, there's the radio." I pointed to a shelf high on the wall across from the beds. The brick wall was painted with the same white paint used on everything else. I shivered remembering all the time I'd spent staring at that wall.

"I knew it was here," I said. My insides clenched up seeing that radio, so I blurted out, "I had the mumps last summer a week after I got here. No one else was sick, and, because I was contagious, I spent almost two weeks in here all alone. Miss Ritz came in to sit with me for a while each day, and either Mrs. Petersen or Miss Nielsen came in and checked on me." I knew I was rambling on and on, but Paul's tight face seemed to be relaxing just a bit, so I kept it up. "Anyway, one of them stopped in every couple of hours. I couldn't reach the radio. One day, before Miss Ritz left, she turned it on to keep me company."

"Being sick here must have been terrible," Paul said.

I nodded. If Paul only knew, he'd really understand terrible, but I'd never tell. I didn't know what made me more embarrassed, wanting Daddy or being scared over a silly commercial in the first place.

Paul reached the radio with barely a stretch being so tall and all. He twisted the black plastic knob on the front to turn it on and rolled the tuner disk on the side slowly searching through the static for a station.

I didn't tell Paul about the commercial that played over and over even though I still remembered every word. First, the creepiest music I'd ever heard oozed around the room followed by the scariest voice. "*The Creature Who Walks Among Us*, the spectacular sequel to *Creature from the Black Lagoon* starring Jeff Morrow as Dr. William Barton." I'd buried my head under the pillow trying to block out the sound, but that never worked. I heard every word. When it stopped, I still heard it in my head over and over again.

A man's serious voice floated out of the small speaker announcing, "*Unshackled*." That voice was nothing compared to the one I could not get out of my head now. Still, Gram had loved that show, so it gave me some comfort.

I remembered feeling ashamed to tell Miss Ritz that those commercials scared me half to death, what with already being twelve and all and the radio up too high for me to turn it off. After I was back in the dormitory, thinking about the awful music kept me awake for hours every night. That's when longing for Daddy was the worst. He should have been alive to protect me from scary commercials and bad dreams.

Paul kept tuning past a saxophone blasting out jazz, Mrs. Petersen's station, and the squeaky voices of The Chipmunks singing their Christmas song. Until, "In today's news . . ."

Our heads almost touched as we tried to catch every word. " . . . a five-alarm fire engulfed most of the school at twenty minutes to three shortly before classes were to be dismissed."

"What school?" Paul shook the little radio making the tuning knob slip off the station.

Alvin The Chipmunk wailed, "I still want a hula hoop . . . "

Paul carefully turned the knob until we heard, " . . . seven units dispatched firemen to the scene. Hundreds to thousands of people have crowded around the blazing building as smoke billows skyward."

Paul's knuckles turned white from his tight grip on the radio. I touched his arm rigid from his pain. Silently, I begged God, *Oh please, please let it not be, please, please, please.*

"A staff member issued this statement, 'May God preserve the lives of our children,' while Sister Mary St. Florence could not be reached."

Paul's face went white. "Sister Mary. Our prin—ci—pal," he choked out, his voice ragged and so quiet I could barely hear him. His shoulders shook as he collapsed to his knees still clutching the radio.

I pried it out of his hands, turned it off and set it on the floor next to the wall. He didn't move. He slumped against the wall with his hands in the shape of the radio. My chest ached. I knew Paul needed Noreen as much as she needed him. I put my hand on his shoulder, but he didn't seem to notice.

"Paul?"

He looked up, his eyes confused and swimming with tears.

"Wait here. I'll get Noreen." Right then, I didn't care anything about rules.

He stared at me blankly.

"Can you wait here? I'll get Noreen."

Paul nodded.

On the way to the Big Girls' Room I didn't stop to think what Mrs. Petersen might say. Paul and Noreen needed each other, and I knew I couldn't take Paul to her. Rushing through the front parlor the thought of Miss Nielsen loomed in my path. Tall and skinny as could be, everyone knew the boy's housemother was dreadfully mean. She never let the boys do anything out of the ordinary. *Please, God, help me do this*, I whispered.

In a few short minutes, I crept back into the infirmary with my arm around Noreen and Sharon in tow. I figured the main reason Sharon had come along was because of Paul being a dreamboat and all, but, one look at her face, and I could tell she was really upset for both Noreen and Paul. Besides, the mascara running down her cheeks, which she was not allowed to own, let alone wear, wasn't going to impress Paul if that's what she was hoping.

Noreen buried her face in her brother's chest, a fresh wave of sobs engulfing them both.

"Shhh," I tried to quiet her. It was a small miracle that we'd made it all the way to the infirmary without anyone seeing us. Silently, I thanked God for the miracle and begged to know what to do next.

That's when the door swung open.

CHAPTER EIGHT

UNRAVELED

Patricia Olsen stepped into the infirmary. Quick as greased lightning, she shut the door and whispered, "What is going on in here?"

"Their old school is on fire," I whispered back.

"No!" Patricia covered her mouth with both hands. "I just finished sweeping the sidewalk. I wondered where all those people rushing down Homan were heading." Her words slipped between her fingers almost too quiet to hear.

Noreen's sobs grew louder.

"Shhh," I whispered. Then I held my breath as if that would make our meeting quieter.

Paul stroked his sister's cheek. So tenderly. Putting his arm around her shoulders, he murmured to her. He focused on her as though his own feelings didn't matter.

"I just knew Noreen had to see her brother." I let my breath escape with my words. "But I don't know what to do now."

"We'll have to get Miss Ritz," Patricia said.

"She's gone," I said. "Paul saw her leave. Maybe she went to see what happened."

Patricia nodded. "Listen. We can't get caught in here. I guarantee you, no matter what, boys and girls roaming about, especially together, will not be tolerated. I can't imagine how you made it here without getting caught." She pressed her fingertips to her forehead and rubbed back and forth.

I couldn't help but notice Patricia had a nice high rounded forehead that did not need bangs to cover it up like my short flat forehead did. I rubbed my eyes. What was wrong with my brain? How awful to think of such a thing now.

"We need a plan." Patricia pressed her fingertips against her forehead. She knew how awful it was to get in trouble at The Home. After she'd moved out of the Big Girls' Room leaving a bed for me, she'd landed a job here working in the kitchen and doing laundry. If we were discovered, she'd be in trouble, too. She might even lose her job. "Here's what we'll do."

Paul and Sharon turned to Patricia. I studied her face.

"First, wait here as quietly as you can," Patricia said. "I'll be right back. I'm going to get the towels I just finished folding."

Sharon and I looked at each other. What in the world did Patricia have in mind? Paul kept his arm around Noreen's shoulders. She was winding down into gulping shaky breaths.

Patricia got back lickety-split with two pink towels and two pink wash cloths folded and stacked. "These are actually Mrs. Petersen's personal towels that she brought from home."

That wasn't a surprise. The towels were pinker than her bedspread and much fluffier than any towels I'd ever seen at The Home.

"Here, Paul." Patricia handed the towels to him. She gave Sharon one of our regular washcloths and pointed at her eyes. Sharon scrubbed at her messy mascara.

Patricia took a deep breath putting her hands on her hips, and, with a determined look on her face, she took control of the situation. "Paul, you take these to Miss Nielsen. Give them to her and immediately go to the Gentlemen's Room."

The Gentlemen's Room? It wasn't the Big Boys' Room? That was odd.

"Don't give her a chance to ask anything," Patricia went on. "But, don't worry, I'm pretty sure she will be thrilled to have them so she won't try very hard to point out the mistake."

Crabby old Miss Nielsen—who was so skinny she had no bosom at all—would be glad to have Mrs. Petersen's fluffy pink towels? That was odder still.

I heard Patricia commenting under her breath, "And, that's a mistake I'm surely going to have to answer for, but, under the circumstances, it can't be helped."

With my thoughts running away like I belonged in a looney bin, I almost missed the next part of Patricia's plan.

"I'm sorry. Really, really, sorry." Patricia had her hand on Noreen's arm. "Go talk to Mrs. Petersen, tell her what happened. She is very good at this kind of thing. Sharon, Debbie, you go along and explain it to her so Noreen won't have to. Then make yourselves scarce until supper time."

Patricia glanced at her watch. "Quarter to six. Only fifteen minutes." Opening the door, she peeked out in both directions. "The coast is clear. Now skedaddle, all of you."

Paul hustled off.

Sharon and I each put an arm around Noreen leading her out of the infirmary.

Patricia followed us closing the door without a sound. "And, please, don't let me catch you in here again," she whispered.

Silently, we made our way to the dormitory one slow step at a time. In the parlor, Noreen stumbled and then stopped dead in her tracks.

"We have to hurry," Sharon whispered. "We need to get back to our room before Mrs. Petersen rings the bell."

Noreen acted as though she didn't hear. With every shaky breath her whole body jerked, and she wasn't focusing on anything around us like she had no idea where she was.

Thinking fast, I whispered, "If we get caught, Paul will get in big trouble."

At that, Noreen began moving. Slowly. I kept my arm around her.

Noreen was sure lucky to have a brother like Paul. Anyone could see, he cared more for her feelings than his own. I wondered if he had made it to his room yet and how Miss Nielsen reacted to the pink towels.

Paul never seemed to care what his housemother thought. He was always getting into trouble. I'd heard that ever since he'd arrived at The Home he'd missed almost every Sunday dinner. He always got in the worst trouble at church.

Every Sunday, we all marched three blocks to Humboldt Park Mission Church on Kedzie. We had two lines, one for the girls and one for the boys. We were always the first ones there filling up the front three rows, girls on the left side of the aisle and boys on the right. The trouble started when the congregation got to the part of the service where everyone was supposed to recite the Lord's Prayer together. Paul refused to say the "for thine is the kingdom, and the power and the glory" part.

Lately, Paul had been yelling "Amen," right after the line "deliver us from evil." That made Miss Nielsen grab him by the ear and drag him back to The Home immediately. I thought it was kind of silly because that's probably exactly what he wanted, except for the ear-pulling part. Noreen said he hated going to a church that wasn't Catholic.

After Paul got kicked out my first week, I kept an eye on him when it got close to the time for the Lord's Prayer. I loved to watch his face, at first all tense and then firm and even courageous. I thought it must look like a soldier going into battle, and I looked forward to it every week. If only I had a brother like that.

Another disappointment was about the singing. I loved to sing, and church was almost my only real opportunity. More than once, one of the old people stopped me after and raved that I sang so beautifully. I wasn't wanting Paul to hear anyone say that, but, every week after he was dragged out, I wished he'd stayed long enough to sing. My mother was a terrific singer and my dad, too. We used to sing together, especially on long car rides, so I'd like to sing with Paul.

"Debbie. Quit daydreaming," Sharon said like it wasn't the first time she'd whispered my name. "I'll check if it's safe, okay?"

I blinked a few times, and the door to the dormitory startled me. We were at the top of the stairs.

Sharon turned the knob like she knew how to sneak around pushing open the door just a crack. With a wave she slipped into the dormitory. After I pushed Noreen in, Sharon closed the door behind us as quiet as a secret.

As we rushed past Mrs. Petersen's room, I could see her turning off her radio and picking up the little brass bell she kept beside it. There was no time now to talk to her privately. I steered Noreen down the aisle to the end by our room passing by Mary Ellen's bed right when Mrs. Petersen started ringing her bell.

"Suppertime," Mrs. Petersen called.

Perfect. If she noticed us, it would only look like we were hungry, so we lined up first.

Mary Ellen set her favorite book on her night table and hopped off her bed to get in line in front of Sharon. I eyed Mrs. Petersen. She waved her bell up and down like always. She probably didn't even know anything about the fire.

Slipping the bell into her apron pocket, Mrs. Petersen said, "Single-file please, girls." Like she did every day. Like nothing devastating had happened to make this day different at all.

"Please bring up the rear, Noreen," she added like Noreen's old school wasn't burning down and all her friends weren't getting hurt. Or worse. I could tell there was no point in asking Mrs. Petersen for help. She'd probably just hug Noreen. That's how she always handled problems. In my opinion, a hug would not be enough. If only Gram were here. She'd know what to do.

Noreen stared at the air in front of her face. Letting all the girls get in line before us, I got behind her to guide her and to make sure she didn't stop along the way. I prayed to know what to do for Noreen and Paul and made up my mind to stop thinking about everything that happened that whole horrible afternoon. I knew God could handle it all better than me.

In the dining hall, every girl and boy had an assigned place for meals. The girls from the Big Girls' Room were always at the table closest to the kitchen. I used to think being the closest to the kitchen meant we'd get our food first. But, it didn't. Every serving dish got to our table last.

No one was allowed to talk in the dining hall except the staff. I watched Noreen while the other kids filed in. She had her eyes glued to the boys' door watching the boys file in and take their seats. Paul came last and took a seat facing the room at the oldest boys' table with his eyes on Noreen the whole time.

The first week I was at the home a boy had said, "Please pass the salt." Miss Nielsen grabbed his ear and sent him up to his dormitory without any supper. It didn't matter what he'd said. The rule was no talking during meals. Period.

But we all knew how to say plenty without talking. Mostly with our eyes. I was an expert at it, so I was sure of what Paul's eyes were saying to his sister. Lifting his eyebrows and pulling them together while pressing his lips into a small smile, he told her he loved her no matter what happened.

It wasn't surprising that Paul didn't bow his head or even close his eyes when Miss Nielsen recited the prayer. Of course, the only reason I knew that was because I didn't close mine either. Miss Nielsen always said the one about God being great and all. To my way of thinking, that was just a nice poem. Not a prayer.

After she prayed, Miss Nielsen hurried to the small dining room for the staff leaving the workers in charge. The housemothers couldn't see us, but they could still hear. If there was any ruckus at all, one of them would rush into the dining hall, and someone ended up going to their dormitory without any supper. Then the workers got scolded for letting it happen.

Only three people worked in the dining hall. Mrs. Bell, who had been the head cook for so many years none of us knew exactly how long. She mostly stayed in the kitchen. The two girls, Patricia and Eileen, helped Mrs. Bell by doing all the serving and cleaning up. It looked like a really crummy job to me, but it was probably the best one either of them could get after growing up in The Home.

Eileen was just plain mean. Maybe because most likely she'd be stuck with that job for the rest of her life because no one would ever be interested in marrying someone who looked like her. She was covered in freckles and had stringy red hair. Her little pig eyes had eyelashes and eyebrows that were such a light color, it looked like she didn't have any at all. Working at The Home sure wasn't the kind of job to make anyone feel like they were doing something worthwhile, so I probably shouldn't feel like she was picking on me when she dropped a baked potato onto my plate. But, did she have to drop it right on top of my creamed corn?

Patricia was always nice. Now that she'd been there for us in the infirmary, I had a whole new respect for her. Plus, with her pretty blonde hair and blue eyes, she wasn't likely to be a worker at The Home for very long. When she came around with pork chops, she took the time to move Noreen's potato and push her corn into a nice pile. She gave Noreen a little smile before she went back to the kitchen.

Noreen stared straight ahead, scooped up a smidgen of food, and slipped it into her mouth like it was any day of the week. She must be tortured inside what with all that was happening to her friends at Our Lady of the Angels, but she looked as calm as a cucumber. How could she do that? Then Noreen glanced down at her lap. I peered over the edge of the table and saw her other hand in her pocket fingering something.

Noreen had her rosary.

CHAPTER NINE

UNCONSOLABLE

Back in our room, Noreen flung herself onto her bed and sobbed into her pillow. I tried patting her back, but she didn't seem to notice. The privacy of our room wasn't so great when I saw how it made Noreen get worse.

"What should we do?" I whispered to Sharon.

Sharon shrugged.

Doing something was better than nothing, so I tugged and yanked until I got Noreen's covers out from under her. Noreen didn't seem to notice that either. Sharon slipped off Noreen's shoes, and we worked together getting her dress off and her nightgown on. We both pulled up the covers and smoothed them over her shaking shoulders. Before I hung up Noreen's dress, I got her rosary out of the pocket and draped it over her clenched fists. I so wanted the touch of those beads to bring Noreen back. But she didn't move a pinch, which meant I had to slide the rosary into the sock in her drawer where it wouldn't get lost.

Without a word, Sharon and I got ready for bed and slipped under our own covers. Gradually Noreen's sobs got quieter until they stopped altogether right before Mrs. Petersen opened the door and found us all in bed. She switched off the light and quietly closed the door.

I blinked my eyes in the dark. Going to sleep, seemed impossible in the empty quiet without the whisper of Noreen fingering her rosary beads, Sharon's steady snoring, and so many awful thoughts to keep me awake. I couldn't keep from thinking of blazing fire, the choking feeling of hot smoke, and the silent sounds of screaming kids. Usually knowing Noreen was praying with her rosary was comforting like I was in on her prayers just by being in the same room. Knowing Noreen felt too awful to even pray was more than I could understand.

It was a long night. No amount of singing hymns in my head or praying, like Gram used to suggest when I couldn't sleep, helped. A shaft of morning sun finally swept across the night table between my bed and Noreen's. Mrs. Petersen's music drifted under the door. I rubbed my face and sat on the edge of my bed exhausted. Sharon stretched her arms wide. Her yawn was loud enough to wake the whole dormitory. But Noreen didn't move. She lay curled up like a baby with her face toward the wall.

I lifted my eyebrows at Sharon.

Sharon shrugged, and we both started getting ready for school.

"By the way, Sharon," I spoke way louder than I needed to hoping Noreen would stir. "Did I ever tell you how much I like that dress?"

"No, you never did," Sharon said. She gave me a puzzled look.

"It makes your eyes look so green," I said directing my voice toward Noreen.

"Thanks," Sharon almost yelled and took a step closer to Noreen. "Your blue dress is jim-dandy."

"Thank you. I did not know you liked it."

The two of us sounded like we were reciting lines from a play that wouldn't last past opening night. But Noreen didn't move.

Sharon leaned over her and shrugged.

I shook Noreen's shoulder as gently as I could. "Noreen," I said. "It's time to get up."

Slowly, Noreen uncurled herself and slid her legs off the bed. When her feet hit the floor, she stood a bit wobbly and reached back to unbutton her nightgown. Sliding off her shoulders, it slipped to the floor. She stood silently as if she didn't know or care that all her underwear was showing.

Staring at her with scared eyes Sharon backed away. "I've got to use the john," she said.

Usually when Sharon said that Noreen pursed her lips and said, "Please, don't use such crude language." This time she looked like she hadn't even heard.

Sharon and I traded worried looks before Sharon hurried off.

It seemed like Noreen was stuck in some kind of private bottomless pit. I grabbed the bent-up black wire hanger from the hook near the foot of Noreen's bed and slipped her dress off it. Helping her get the dress on was like dressing one of the stiff dolls in the playroom. When Noreen slumped onto the bed, I kept her upright. Sitting close to keep her from flopping over, I pulled on her socks. Sharon got back. She put on Noreen's shoes and tied them.

"Let me help with your hair," I said hoping Noreen would respond. She kept staring ahead at nothing. Brushing it gently, I tried my best to make her hair lay correctly. What with Noreen keeping her face to the wall all night, she'd managed to make one side want to stick straight up. The only solution to get it anywhere near right without drenching it with water was a good spit and swipe, plus, three bobby pins.

Between the two of us, Sharon and I managed to get Noreen downstairs to breakfast. Eileen slopped slimy oatmeal into bowls for everyone. I covered it with way more brown sugar than was allowed in order to force it down.

While I was scooping extra brown sugar onto Noreen's oatmeal, Miss Ritz showed up. She went directly to Paul and squatted down next to his chair. They talked quietly for a few minutes until the two of them came and got Noreen. Taking his sister's hand, Paul never took his eyes off her and didn't see Sharon mouth "good morning." I kept my lips still since clearly there was nothing good about this morning after yesterday.

Later at school, Doris waited, as usual, leaning against our Maple tree near the door closest to Homan Avenue. "Did you hear?" she asked before I even got all the way there.

"Uh-huh."

Doris looked surprised. Most of the time I didn't know about anything that was going on outside The Home. We hardly ever watched television, and no one had their own radio.

"I don't know any kids who went to Our Lady, but it is awful." Her words hung in the air making my silence awkward.

Even with my eyes open I could still see Noreen's face pressed against Paul's chest. And Noreen all curled up in bed. And Noreen's nightgown in a puddle around her feet on the gray tile floor of our room. But I couldn't put it all into words. I couldn't find the right ones, so I nodded and swallowed trying to hold back tears.

"I heard eighty-seven kids died, but only three nuns," Doris said. "That doesn't seem right."

I stared past our Maple into nothing. Doris put her hand on my arm and didn't say another word which is what a real friend does. Even when she might have plenty of questions and opinions to share.

In class, Mr. Kelly stood in front of the room waiting until we all took our seats. "I am sorry to say," he said making a sad face. "We will not be having a Christmas concert this year."

A buzz of whispers ran around the room.

With a small frown, Mr. Kelly explained that the music teacher, Mrs. O'Hare had taken a leave of absence. Her daughter had attended Our Lady of the Angels school, but he didn't tell us what happened to Mrs. O'Hare's daughter.

My throat squeezed shut. It didn't matter anymore that Mrs. O'Hare never noticed how much I loved to sing. Or how Roberta's voice sounded dreadfully weak, but she still got a part to sing for the Christmas concert. Or that Doris was furious because I should have been picked. All that mattered now was the fire and how it had ruined so many lives.

Mr. Kelly's announcement subdued the whole class, and, somehow, I got through the rest of the day without crying. Right after lunch, Mr. Kelly left the room, probably to go to the washroom, leaving Roberta in charge. When he got back, she didn't tell him "the girl from that Home," left her seat to use the dictionary while he was gone.

I knew Mr. Kelly didn't like it when my book slid to the floor during American History. Or when my pencil rolled off my desk twice during Arithmetic. Or when he frowned at my third request to go to the restroom. I didn't even realize I'd been sighing over and over, until he pointed it out and assigned the sentences. I only got up to use the dictionary to find out what the word "erratic" meant since it was part of the sentence I had to write a hundred times tonight. I couldn't deny that my behavior had been "deviating from the usual or proper course in conduct" most of the day.

"No matter what happens in life, self-control is a necessity," he'd said.

Which sounded an awful lot like being still to me.

When I got back to The Home, I sat on my bed writing my sentence one hundred times. "I will not indulge myself with erratic behavior regardless of my circumstances." I kept one eye on the door waiting for Sharon and, hopefully, Noreen.

Mr. Kelly loved assigning sentences that took up more than one line. Today when I'd been assigned the sentences, I saw Doris' face. She was mad, but, today, I didn't care. Writing sentences seemed trivial now.

In the Big Girls' Room, I was glad to do them to keep my mind busy. Finishing the first page, twenty-eight lines, fourteen sentences, I started on the next page. I wrote "I will not" at the beginning of every other line, until the door burst open.

"She's not here?" Sharon rushed into the room. "She wasn't at school all day either."

I jumped up. "But, then where could she be?"

We stared at each other until our eyes filled with tears and spilled over. I reached out to Sharon. She flopped down next to me and the two of us clung to each other. I couldn't stop thinking what it must be like to be in a fire or to know someone who was. The tears I'd held inside for so long wouldn't stop.

I peered out to the dormitory through our open door and my tears. The other girls were sitting quietly on their beds holding a book or openly staring into the Big Girls' Room. Leaping up, I slammed the door shut. I wiped my cheeks with my arm and then my nose started running. Noreen was the one who always had a hanky ready in case someone needed it.

A few moments later, Mrs. Petersen peeked in the door. "Are you girls all right?" And then she was in the room hugging us both at the same time and murmuring, "It's okay, it's okay."

Sharon was the first to pull away. "Where's Noreen?"

"She's fine, my dear. As fine as she can be right now." Mrs. Petersen patted my back.

"But where is she?" I needed to know.

"Noreen and her brother are staying in the infirmary tonight, dear." Mrs. Petersen laid her hand on my shoulder.

"When will she be back?"

"But, what about school?" Sharon interrupted. "I didn't see her all day."

"She'll be back," Mrs. Petersen said. "Soon. Now, you two go wash up. It's almost supper time."

In the washroom, both of us splashed cold water on our eyes and cheeks over and over, until our faces in the mirrors looked almost normal. Patting mine dry without unfolding my towel, I heard the little brass bell and Mrs. Petersen's "supper time."

With our arms around each other's shoulder, Sharon and I joined the end of the line.

CHAPTER TEN

UNWELCOME

Noreen didn't come back soon. She was gone on Wednesday and Thursday, too. After Sharon got home from school Thursday, Mrs. Petersen came into the Big Girls' Room and closed the door behind her.

"Tomorrow, Miss Ritz will be taking Noreen and her brother to the funeral," she told us. She explained that Noreen and Paul knew many of the kids who died and all three of the nuns.

I pressed my lips against my teeth but not to hold in any laughing. I hadn't felt like laughing at all since Monday, and it seemed like I never would.

"We all need to be patient with Noreen. Don't ask her about the—" Mrs. Petersen stopped and swallowed like it was hard to go on. "Fire. Wait for her to bring it up. I expect she'll be grieving for a long time."

I didn't sleep much at all on any of those nights. Horrible fiery images flashed in my thoughts so real that I was afraid to go to sleep. And, it was still too quiet without the soft murmurs of Noreen's prayers. Not to mention the lack of Sharon's snoring, which proved neither of us got much rest.

On Saturday, when Sharon and I got back to the Big Girls' Room after supper, Noreen was curled up on her bed.

"Hi, Noreen," Sharon said.

I patted Noreen's shoulder and said, "Hi."

Noreen rolled over. She gave us a small smile, but I could see there was nothing anywhere near a smile in her eyes. Her eyes held so much sadness, I could barely look at her. And, I had no idea what I should say to her? If Noreen was back, Paul must be, too. He could tell me what to say to Noreen. I decided to sneak downstairs to find him. Everyone was so busy right after supper I figured it would be easy. Besides, after our "sneak" to the infirmary I felt a whole new confidence about going where I wanted when I wanted. There really wasn't an official rule forbidding us to leave our rooms, but, for some reason, we were all afraid to, and Miss Nielsen had a lot to do with that fear.

I made it all the way to the hallway by the infirmary without so much as a hint of where Paul could be. I decided to head back. He must be in his room acting like nothing had happened, just like Noreen. Stepping into the parlor, I heard voices coming from the girls' stairs that led to the dining hall.

" . . . most of the day off. Looks like your wish came true." It sounded like Mrs. Bell. But who was she talking to?

"All her wishes come true," Eileen said with her usual snarl.

"That's not so," Patricia said.

"Seems to me like they do."

"Girls, please," Mrs. Bell said. "You'll both be glad of this news. On the Sunday after Valentine's Day, we will not need to prepare dinner or serve at all. But you mustn't tell any of the children."

Mustn't tell? A secret? I scooted closer to the stairs and perked up my ears.

"Where will everyone be?" Patricia asked.

"Miss Ritz has decided to plan an event."

"Sounds like extra cooking and serving to me," Eileen said interrupting.

"Not this time. It's to be an outing for all the children."

"How wonderful!" Patricia said.

"Miss Ritz is enlisting all the churches nearby to get folks to sign up to take a child out for the afternoon," Mrs. Bell said. "It's a way for them to think of doing something good for orphans. But, mind you, we will be serving breakfast before church." The kitchen door banged shut.

I could hear Eileen's grumbling, but I couldn't make out any more words. Hope grew in my heart like a pink bubble of Bazooka gum.

An outing. Folks who cared for orphans were coming to take us out? Folks who liked children and maybe wanted a child. My chest swelled up with hope. Was God answering my prayers for a new family?

More importantly, maybe this outing would give Noreen something to hope for. Or maybe not. Noreen had Paul, and she would be a nun soon enough, so she probably didn't care to have a new family. I wondered what Sharon would say? No matter what I knew, telling Sharon and Noreen wasn't a good idea at all. I wasn't telling anyone. It was supposed to be a secret. A secret that could make my biggest wish come true. I was just sure of it.

Gram would have been proud of me thinking of someone else's feelings like she's always told me, a sure sign I was starting to put others first or at least a quick second.

The next day no one laughed or did anything louder than a whisper. On Saturday night after supper, I finished up my homework a few minutes after the dormitory lights went out. Tiptoeing into the washroom, I brushed my teeth and then my hair. Back in the Big Girls' Room, Noreen and Sharon were already in bed when I slipped under my covers. Sharon held a paperback book reading silently, but Noreen curled up with her face toward the wall.

The door swung open, and, before I could blink, Sharon had her book under her pillow.

Mrs. Petersen stood at the doorway. "I'm pleased you girls are ready for lights out a little early. All of you need your sleep." She switched off the light and closed the door.

Framed by the window over Sharon's bed, the moon was a Cheshire cat's smile. A thought like that usually made me feel like laughing, something that room hadn't heard in what seemed like forever. I used to think laughing was always the best thing to do, but now I knew better.

The unique whisper of Noreen's fingers moving along her rosary beads usually put me to sleep. It felt like I'd never hear that again. Now, steady, low breathing drifted through the dark room. Maybe Noreen had escaped to a deep sleep. I hoped it was so.

"Debbie?" Sharon whispered so softly I barely heard it.

"What?"

"I've been dying—" Sharon whispered. "Oops, sorry, I shouldn't say it like that. I mean, I've been wanting to ask you a favor, but with Noreen and all it didn't seem right, don't ya know."

Oh no! Had Sharon been struggling with something awful, afraid to tell me when our room was already filled to the brim with sadness? "I think Noreen's asleep. What is it?"

"On Saturday nights some kids from school meet up at the park."

Relief poured over me like ointment on a burn. Sharon sounded so alive and excited; it was plain good to think about something that wasn't sad.

"How could you ever go?"

"I already figured that out," Sharon said. "There's a delivery door in the storage room."

When had Sharon been sneaking around?

"I never knew that," I whispered.

"I found it last night after everyone was asleep."

"Really?"

"Sure. Mrs. Petersen is asleep by ten o'clock, don't ya know," Sharon said. "If you go down to the dining hall and through the kitchen, it's right there."

"I don't think this is a good idea."

"Why not?"

"It's just wrong."

"Don't you ever wonder what the kids at school do when they go home?"

"Actually no," I said. But now I wondered why I never did.

The moon's smile outside the window caught my attention. Shimmering so far off in the distance, it could make a girl wonder about a lot of things.

"Well I have. Every other girl in my class has friends who come over every day after school and you know what they do? They listen to 45s. And drink Coke. And watch TV whenever they want to. All the girls at school go out on Saturday nights. They never let us do anything in this place. It's not fair."

"Well . . . " I didn't know what to say. Sharon's list made me want a new family more than ever, so I could get out of here. Surely the out- ing would be my ticket. But I didn't understand why Sharon was even telling me about sneaking out. Why didn't she just do it?

"I would have waited for you to go to sleep," Sharon hesitated and then barreled on, "but, I need your help."

I didn't answer right away. I couldn't blame Sharon for wanting to go out like all the other girls at school. Then again, if I helped Sharon and either one of us got caught, we'd both be in trouble. Big trouble. "Why do you need me?"

"The delivery door locks when it closes. And, it's tricky to open so I need to show you how to do it." Sharon paused and then went on in a rush, "Because I need you to let me back in."

Sharon had never asked me for a favor before, and it was hard to say no like I knew I should. It didn't seem worth the risk to me. I was about to tell her as much when one word sailed across the dark room.

"Please?"

CHAPTER ELEVEN

UNSETTLED

Even though I knew it was a bad idea, I swung my legs off my bed and crept over to Sharon's bed. "Okay, I'll do it." Maybe I was too tired and too sick of being sad to think straight.

Sharon pulled back her covers and got up fully dressed. When did she do that? She immediately started arranging her pillow and pulling up her covers making it look like she was under them. I fixed my bed the same and got out my favorite red plaid flannel blouse, the one I put in the laundry only when I absolutely had to. Pulling it on over my blue pajamas, I buttoned it and knotted the tails at my waist.

When Sharon tugged on my arm and made a hurry-up face, I left my shoes behind. It would be easier to be quiet without them. No one would see me anyway, so it wouldn't matter. But I did snatch the book Doris had borrowed from Mr. Kelly for me since he wouldn't let me take books overnight because of where I lived.

We tiptoed through the dormitory and past Mrs. Petersen's room. Sharon turned the doorknob to the stairway, and it sent out a squeak that seemed way louder than all the sleeping girls put together. I froze. But, no one moved so we snuck out and down the stairs. We managed to make it down to the dining hall with barely another sound. I could still smell the beef stew we'd had for supper.

Sharon stopped and slipped on her brown penny loafers. The ones she'd told Noreen and me were a special gift from her mother before she died in a sanatorium. Her mother had put dimes in the penny slots, so "her daughter would always feel rich."

Seeing those dimes made me feel sorry for Sharon. I followed her through the kitchen thinking how much she deserved a little fun.

"See, I told you there's a door here," Sharon said opening the delivery door. A stiff wind blew in along with a few stray leaves. My feet were so cold I wished I had my shoes.

"But, it's tricky. You have to push in on the handle to get it to open. Try it." Sharon shoved the door shut with her hip.

With a push, I tried to twist the knob, but it wouldn't budge. I twisted the handle again and pushed harder until it finally opened.

"When will you be back?" I asked.

"I'll be back in a jiff."

"When's that?" I knew Sharon's idea of a jiff and mine were worlds apart.

"Relax," Sharon said. "You don't need to worry, everything's copacetic."

"I need to know when to let you in."

"Fiddlesticks. I didn't think of that," Sharon said looking at me. But her eyes slipped up to the right, a sure sign she was lying.

I knew this was a bad idea. But, how could I say that now? Looking around the storage room, I tried to figure out what to do. Green beans, corn, and even pancake syrup stared back at me. The huge cans filled up the floor-to-ceiling shelves painted white of course. I wanted to say I changed my mind, but one look at Sharon, and I knew I couldn't disappoint her now.

"You need to be back in an hour," I said.

"An hour?" Sharon put her hands on her hips like she was going to insist on more time.

I glanced around the room. "Surely, you can see there isn't even a place for me to sit here."

Sharon glanced at her watch. "Okey-doke, that'll be plenty of time," she said so quickly it was silly of me to trust her.

Before I could say anything, Sharon slipped out the door and up the concrete steps. I watched her scurry to the alley and disappear without so much as a wave of thanks. Closing the door, I checked in the kitchen and found an old wooden chair needing a coat of that white paint and carried it back to the storage room. Sitting, I pulled my feet up and rubbed them.

Opening my book, I heard a squeaky thunk. What was that? I listened for more and tiptoed into the kitchen. A dim light made a rectangle around the swinging door to the dining hall. I held my breath and waited. A chair scraped.

Now what?

Peeking into the crack of weak light, the dining hall looked dark, but not too dark to see someone sitting at a table. The oldest boys' table. Who could it be? Someone else who was sneaking around that was for sure. I knew it wasn't an adult, so I took a breath and barged right through the doorway.

It was Paul.

Thank goodness. Trying to sound like I ran into people wearing my pajamas and barefoot every night I said, "Whatcha doing?"

"Reading."

Paul pointed at a book he had propped up on the table and didn't seem surprised at all to see me. He had a black flashlight balanced on his shoulder directed to the cover lighting up a picture of a dog and the title.

"*Old Yeller*, I've read that."

Paul didn't look up. "Me, too. But it's the only book I could find tonight."

What an odd thing to say. This must not be the first time he's been here after lights out.

Paul glanced up from the page. Even in the dim light I could see the strain on his face. With a smile, I slipped onto the chair across the table from him and opened *Gone Away Lake*. This is what Gram would call a golden opportunity; meaning, God must have had something to do with it. Ever since Monday, I'd so wanted to let Paul know I cared about Noreen and him.

Moonlight streamed in from the short window at the top of the wall behind me scarcely enough to see by. I read the first page twice. I still didn't understand what Portia Blake and her brother Foster were doing. Seemed like there was no point in figuring that out, now. Gram also said, "Never let a golden opportunity slip by."

"I'm sorry," I said quickly before I chickened out. "I can't even imagine how you must feel, or Noreen either, but I'm really sorry."

"Thanks."

"I wish I knew what to say," I said.

"There's nothing to say."

"I know . . . but I thought, maybe, you could tell me if there's something I can do for Noreen."

Paul closed his book. Using both hands, he aimed his flashlight toward the ceiling making soft shadows fall across his face. The saddest face I had ever seen. Even sadder than Noreen's. Seeing it made my chest hurt.

"It wasn't in church."

I knew he meant the funeral. Having a church funeral was important to Catholics.

"None of the caskets were open. I was glad of that."

What could I say? Nothing. So, I listened.

"But there were so many of them. Small and white. Too small. And all lined up in rows." A single tear rolled down his cheek and hung on his chin for a moment before it dripped off. Paul didn't seem to notice; he just went on. "The armory was packed with people. Parents holding onto brothers and sisters. Reporters scribbling in notebooks. Priests whispering prayers. Nuns clutching their rosaries. Even the Cardinal came. People all over the place were crying, and cameras kept flashing everywhere. I hated the cameras. It wasn't a time for cameras."

Paul clenched the flashlight tighter making the beam of light flit across the low ceiling.

"When we were looking for a seat, Carolyn Sullivan came out of nowhere and grabbed Noreen around the middle sobbing. She's only seven. Her sister, Maureen, was Nor's best friend. Until we came here." His chin trembled.

I hadn't realized all their friends dying reminded them of their parents dying, too. But, now, I could tell it was so.

"Carolyn's father pried her off Nor just as a woman with a camera was ready to take a picture of them."

"I'd hate the cameras, too," I whispered.

"We finally found some empty chairs. A man, I don't know who, read every name. It took a long, long time. When they said—" Paul stopped.

I watched his Adam's apple bob down and back up.

"When they said Maureen Sullivan, Noreen broke down. She couldn't stop crying. Her whole body was shaking like she couldn't control it, and she started gasping for breath. Miss Ritz had to shake her.

"After all the names were read, the Archbishop sang High Mass. When it was over, soldiers carried the caskets out. Families followed each one. We just sat there. I didn't want to follow just one of them. Finally,

Miss Ritz put her arm around Noreen and made us leave. We never saw Carolyn or any of her family again. There were too many people."

Paul let the flashlight slip to the table and buried his face in his arms. The flashlight rolled toward the edge. I caught it before it fell. Paul didn't make a sound, but his shoulders heaved up and down. Up and down. I let him be for as long as I could stand it. Then I got up and put my hand on his shoulder making him heave even more. I patted his back, and he looked up. "It's just too much, Mom and Dad and now this . . . and I have to be strong. The man in the family . . . for Noreen." His eyes were red with tears streaming down making his whole face wet.

"You are strong. Exactly like a grown-up man."

Paul slowly wiped his sleeve over his face and rubbed his eyes. Finally, he took a deep breath that was only a bit shaky. "Thanks. I feel better now. And, I can do it. Be strong for both of us. I can be the man of our family."

Neither one of us moved.

Paul wiped his face again.

With the saddest sigh I've ever heard, he picked up his flashlight and book. "I'm really tired," he said and trudged over to the boys' stairs.

Had I missed an opportunity? I never reminded him how much Jesus loves him or anything. I only listened. Maybe that's what he needed what with being sad and all. He hadn't even acted surprised to see me, and I didn't think he realized it was the middle of the night, or that we were in the dining hall sitting at the same table.

A flash of Gram kneeling beside her bed filled my mind making me close my eyes to pray. *Dear God, please comfort Paul and Noreen. And,* in my heart, I knew He would.

CHAPTER TWELVE

UNACCEPTABLE

After Paul left, I tried to read, but it was too dark, and I didn't really care to read. Not after seeing Paul like that. So, instead, I laid my head on my arms and prayed.

I woke with a start, but it took a moment to remember where I was and why. Loud knocking reminded me. Jumping up, I ran to the storage room and grabbed the door knob.

"Shhh," I shushed pushing the knob hard to get the door open.

Sharon burst in. "I've been knocking for an hour."

I didn't believe her for a red-hot minute. Sharon would never be that patient.

It was dark walking through the kitchen, but I could still make out the time on the clock above the two refrigerators standing side by side. It was way after midnight. "Hey. It's after twelve-thirty. You were supposed to be back in an hour. That would have been eleven-thirty."

"I lost track of time." Sharon was already halfway through the kitchen. "I can't do this anymore."

"Don't worry," Sharon said with a catch in her voice. "I'm not going out again." Without another word, she shoved open the swinging door.

I got through on the same swing and caught her arm. "Wait a minute," I said. I knew we couldn't talk once we got back to our room or we might wake Noreen, and I deserved an explanation. "What happened?"

"You wouldn't understand." Sharon's voice sounded strange. "You're too young."

"I was old enough to help you sneak out."

Sharon flinched at the word *sneak*. She opened her mouth. Closed it. Finally, like a knocked over bottle of Coke, she started spilling it out. "Well, if you have to know, when I got to the monkey bars where we were supposed to all meet, only two boys were there and one girl, but she was on the very top of the monkey bars. I was late, so I was surprised Veronica wasn't there yet. I thought she was my best friend. At first, I figured she would show up any minute, but she never did."

"What did you do?" I asked

"We all talked and stood around. The girl, I think her name is Marion, was all chrome-plated and stayed up on the monkey bars. One of the boys kept trying to get her to come down. Everyone knows he thinks he's a smooth operator. I kept wondering what was taking Veronica—" Sharon stopped in the middle of her sentence. Even in the dim light I could see she was ready to cry.

"So . . . " I prompted.

"After a long time and a lot of kidding around, Marion climbed down. One of the boys, the smooth operator, snuggled up to her right away, and . . . then I knew why they were all there. But, that's not for me. I got out of there as fast as I could."

"They didn't follow you?"

"No. The other boy kept whistling and calling me back, but I ignored him and went faster. I could hear them all laughing at me." Sharon covered her face and started crying. "And, I was really scared."

I put my arm around her. "I'm sorry."

Pretty quickly, Sharon stopped crying and pulled a hanky out of her coat pocket. Wiping her eyes and face she said, "I'm sorry I tried to lie to you."

"I forgive you." I still wasn't sure she'd told me the whole story. "But, you're okay, right?"

"I am," Sharon said.

"Really?"

"I learned my lesson that's for sure." She blew her nose. "No more sneaking out for me." Stuffing her hanky back into her coat pocket she gave me a shaky grin. "Come on, let's go to bed."

Back in the Big Girls' Room, the sound of Noreen's breathing filled the air, even though her face was to the wall. We both got in bed really quickly. I thought I'd never fall asleep with so much to think about. Paul and Noreen, Sharon's close call and seeing that door. A girl could escape after all. But, there still would be no place to go.

The next morning Paul held Noreen's hand on the way to church, and no one said anything about it. He led her to a seat on the aisle and sat right across from her watching her the whole time. When everyone said the Lord's Prayer, he didn't get in trouble. He was still there when we got to the singing. But I couldn't hear him, and I didn't see his lips move. Maybe he didn't like singing or maybe his heart was too heavy. Either way, I found myself whispering the words. It didn't seem right to enjoy anything anymore.

Sunday night, Noreen's almost silent fingers on her rosary beads put me to sleep. I was so glad she'd started to pray again. Right before I drifted off, I heard Sharon snoring, too.

At school on Monday, three men in overalls went from room to room throughout the whole building. They took off the doors in each room and put them back on in a way that made them swing out into the hallway instead of into the room. They rehung the entrance doors too. Mr. Kelly read a newspaper article that explained how safe the school would be now.

Then he showed another boring filmstrip. Where in the world did he ever find so many films about the war? I couldn't even laugh at them anymore. The sadness that hung in the air like black crepe didn't make Mr. Kelly any nicer to me, but I didn't care.

At supper, Patricia and Eileen served up meatloaf, green beans, and mashed potatoes. I smiled over at Mary Ellen. Then I made an awful face at the mashed potatoes, but Eileen was on to me and gave Sharon two huge scoops.

"Guess you're in luck, missy," Eileen said, in her meanest voice. "Seems we're out of potatoes. Looks like you won't be getting any at all." She tipped the bowl so I could see it was empty and sashayed herself back to the kitchen.

Sharon scooted her plate next to mine and slid half the potatoes over. They were delicious. Even though she'd probably never admit it, I could tell Sharon cared for me more than she ever did before last Saturday night. Both of us would probably always be better friends now.

When we got in line to follow the other girls upstairs, Eileen, balancing a tall stack of plates, shoved her shoulder against the kitchen door. "Over two months till we finally get a break," she said, grumbling.

Turning away quick as a wink, I picked up my pace.

Sharon grabbed my shoulder. "What was that about?"

"How should I know?" My voice rose to a squeak and my cheeks burned with a blush.

"You're keeping something from me," Sharon said.

I could tell she didn't like it one bit.

CHAPTER THIRTEEN

UNDISCIPLINED

Upstairs, a girl I'd never seen before stood in the aisle of the dormitory. Beside her, Mrs. Petersen wore a frazzled look, her eyes searching around the room. She shuffled the bedding she held into one arm and put the other arm around the new girl.

With a snotty look, the girl twisted out from under our kind-hearted housemother's arm.

Mrs. Petersen fumbled in her apron pocket and found her little bell. Ringing it seemed to settle her a bit. "Girls. This is Beverly Jensen," Mrs. Petersen announced nodding at the new girl. "She's ten and in the fifth grade."

Beverly stood ramrod straight looking like a fancy broomstick in her brown velvet dress. Her long skinny braids hung like blonde arrows pointing to her shiny Mary Janes with two straps and pure white anklets. She was taller than any ten-year-old I'd ever seen. Maybe almost as tall as me.

Usually new girls had a place all set up for them when they arrived. It looked like Beverly came in a bit of a hurry. Mrs. Petersen searched around the whole room a second time and then heaved her shoulders in a big sigh. She stepped over to the only empty bed in the room, right next to Mary Ellen's. "This isn't the best choice . . ."

"What?" Beverly pressed her lips together looking every bit the haughty princess. "Where is my room?"

I prayed silently. Please, please, don't let her be put in the Big Girls' Room.

"Well, um, dear, um," Mrs. Petersen stuttered. "Here the, um, girls share this nice big room. Nancy and Diane are both in fifth grade just like you. Their beds are right over there." She pointed right across the aisle.

"Nice?" Beverly crossed her arms with a scathing look on her face.

Several girls gasped. Apparently, this girl didn't have a clue about how things worked at The Home. Nancy and Diane stood between their beds, arms wrapped around each other. They were best friends. Everyone knew it would be awful to separate them.

"Well! I certainly cannot sleep next to a baby," Beverly proclaimed lifting her chin. Her snotty stare swept the room and stopped on Mary Ellen sitting on the edge of her bed only two feet from the empty one.

Mrs. Petersen peered around the room again as if she thought another bed would suddenly appear. "Okay then," she said giving Beverly one of her trying-to-be-stern looks. "We'll have to make do here. Let's get you settled now." She laid the bedding on the empty bed.

I eyed Beverly. I did not like the look of this new girl and especially what she said about Mary Ellen. Or how she said it. No one was getting away with that if I could help it. Mary Ellen wasn't a baby, but she was too little to look out for herself. Besides, she felt like family even if she wasn't, so I decided then and there I would be sure to keep a close watch on Mary Ellen. And an eagle eye on this Beverly.

Sharon breezed down the aisle to the Big Girls' Room. I followed, but I didn't miss how the new girl narrowed her eyes and watched us the whole way.

In our room, Sharon pulled the door shut and turned to me. "So?"

I glanced at the empty bed across from Sharon's. "Maybe we should have reminded Mrs. Petersen about—"

"That girl is surely going to be trouble. She'd never put her in here now. Not with," Sharon paused for a moment and then stumbled on. "Noreen and all."

"It might be better," I said thinking aloud. "For the younger girls."

"Who cares?" Sharon waved her hand like she was waving my concerns away. "As long as she's not in here, she can't bother us."

"You're right," I said. "But I feel sorry for all the girls in the dorm, especially Mary Ellen."

"That little snot will have a heyday with her." Sharon flopped onto her bed, slid her book out from her pillow, but, before she started reading, she squinted her eyes in my direction and asked, "Why do you care so much for Mary Ellen?"

Caught off guard, I quickly pulled open my drawer and started rummaging around in it. "It's just that she's the youngest here," I said trying to sound like Mary Ellen wasn't special to me at all. I could never admit to Sharon that I liked to pretend Mary Ellen is my little sister. Lucky for me, Sharon was reading her book.

The door opened letting in the sound of Beverly's screechy voice. "I cannot believe this."

I caught a glimpse of the dormitory where Mrs. Petersen was putting the sheets on Beverly's bed for her. I figured she was showing her how, but it looked to me like Beverly had no intention of learning. She wasn't even watching.

Noreen scooted in and closed the door behind her fast.

Sharon closed her book and sat up. "Hi, Noreen," she said.

I don't think Noreen heard her. Sharon gave me a frown that turned into a glare quicker than a whistle. "Hey, I still want to know what Eileen was talking about."

I stalled. Wishing more than ever that I could keep the idea of a new family to myself. I looked at Noreen for help. She didn't notice or seem to be listening. She had an Algebra book open on her lap.

Sharon acted like she might wring the information out of me if she had to, glaring at me with both hands on her hips.

I pointed my face at Noreen and lifted my eyebrows as if to say, "I'm not saying anything with Noreen listening."

Sharon cleared her throat.

Noreen looked up with a confused look on her face. "I need to use the ladies' room," she said.

As soon as the door was closed, I took a deep breath and said. "All I heard was Mrs. Bell giving Patricia and Eileen some instructions." If only I could think fast and come up with a quick lie like I knew Sharon could.

"Instructions for what?" Sharon said. "With the way you acted, I know it was way more than ordinary instructions."

"But, I can't—I can't say anything. It's a big huge secret."

Sharon clamped her lips together and glared at me.

"Okay," I said. "I heard Mrs. Bell tell Patricia and Eileen not to tell any of us. I really hate how they do that. Never telling us anything." I kept stalling for time and for a good idea of what to say. I didn't want to tell Sharon or anyone so I could hold the thought of Miss Ritz's plan in my heart. I'd been praying over and over for a family to take me out and like me so much they'd want me to be theirs for good.

"Just tell me already."

I couldn't think of anything Sharon would believe, which meant I didn't have a choice except to tell her the truth. "You can't tell anyone else," I said.

"What kinda drip do you think I am?" Sharon made a face like she was insulted at the thought. "I won't tell a soul, don't ya know."

"Promise?"

"Cross my heart and hope to die." Sharon made a big X on her chest with her finger. "Or I'll stick a needle in my eye."

Even with that Sharon didn't really seem like the trustworthy type. I glared into her eyes long and hard reminding myself how wrong it was to lie or tell a secret. I didn't want to tell, but I knew it was mostly because the secret outing had become my secret. I hated lying, and my mind was so full of hope I couldn't think past the truth anyway. "Okay." I sighed. "Miss Ritz is organizing an outing."

"For us?" Sharon asked. "Nifty."

For a moment, I thought I wouldn't have to tell the rest, but she crossed her arms and gave me a glare. I knew if I didn't tell her everything I'd have to lie, too. Gram was surely right when she told me to never eavesdrop.

"Okay. So, I heard Mrs. Bell telling Eileen and Patricia they won't have to work after church on the Sunday after Valentine's Day. It's because of the fire," I said. Saying that made my throat swell up.

Sharon looked confused.

"Since everyone is so upset about that," I said. "They might have a soft spot for orphans because Valentine's Day is all about loving each other. At least that's why I think she planned it."

"O-h," Sharon said like that made sense to her.

"So, Miss Ritz is inviting people from all over the neighborhood to come and take us out, on that Sunday afternoon."

"Wow! Sounds like the living end." Sharon was getting excited.

"It sounded like each of us will be going with a couple like a mom and a dad. Maybe especially couples who, you know, families who—" I stopped and glanced at the door. "You know, families who lost children."

Sharon's eyebrows flew up at that. "Double wow!" She twirled around the room landing on her bed. "But, where're we gonna go?"

"I'm not sure. It sounded like we get to go out for the whole afternoon."

"Hunky-dory!"

I didn't say we'll get a chance to feel like part of a family. At least I could keep that to myself.

"Do you think they'll take us shopping? I'd love to go shopping at Marshall Field's!"

"Sharon," I said shocked. "That's awful! No one mentioned shopping. They're taking us out to dinner, isn't that enough for you?"

Noreen slipped in the door. She didn't say a word as she lay down on her bed with her face to the wall. Sharon went back to her book reading, and I opened *Gone Away Lake,* but the words were blurry because of the tears that filled my eyes. If only the Sunday after Valentine's day could make everything perfect for Noreen and Paul, too.

CHAPTER FOURTEEN

UNRULY

The next morning, we could all see Beverly was a completely spoiled brat. I didn't pay any attention to her. Not even when she complained about the lack of fresh clothes to wear. Or, when she ignored the no talking rule in the dining hall, and Mrs. Petersen had to come in the dining hall twice to shush her because she refused to eat pancakes without sausage and bacon. And, certainly not when she said the walk to school was much too far.

With Beverly and her meanness sleeping right next to Mary Ellen, I got a hold of my little sister's hand on the way out the girls' door and held it all the way to school. I didn't care if Beverly or Roberta or anyone else said anything. When we got there, Doris stood waiting by our Maple, looking surprised that I wasn't alone. I gave her a just-a-sec look and squatted down to make sure I had Mary Ellen's attention.

"After school, if you get out before I do," I said. "Wait for me right here."

Mary Ellen nodded.

"A new girl arrived at The Home yesterday," I said to Doris with my lips tight and my eyebrows flexed.

"I saw a new girl this morning," Doris said. "Was she wearing a bright red coat with a black lambswool collar?"

"That was Beverly," Mary Ellen said. "Isn't her coat beautiful? She has a velvet dress, and did you see how long her hair is?"

"I did." Doris smiled at Mary Ellen and patted her head.

I never told Doris that Mary Ellen is like a little sister to me, but she knew we had a special connection.

"Go get in line with the first graders now," I said. "I'll see you right after school."

As soon as she was out of earshot, Doris blurted out, "I'd never have guessed that girl was from The Home. I saw her bump into a little boy and knock him right down, but she didn't stop or act like she noticed. She went right into school like she was the Queen of Sheba or something. Before the bell even rang."

"Sounds just like her," I said. "She's rude to everyone."

At the end of the day, I watched my classmates file out of the classroom while I waited in the last seat of row six again. Would Mary Ellen be okay waiting for me? I kept every part of me as still as a soldier at attention, but Mr. Kelly took his sweet time anyway. He erased the board and then carefully wrote, Tuesday, December 16, 1958, before he told me to write, "I will mind my own business and stop daydreaming during class." All because Roberta had tattled on me when he'd left the room.

I'd only gotten out of my seat for a few seconds to help Doris look up "demonstrate" in the dictionary. I knew it was a hard word to find if a girl thought the "o" in the middle was an "e." If only Mr. Kelly would write the spelling words on the blackboard like most teachers did instead of reading the list. It would be a lot easier.

Today, before the word "dismissed" was all the way out of Mr. Kelly's mouth, I hightailed it out of there. Fumbling with my stack of books and trying to get my coat on in a hurry, I prayed Mary Ellen was still waiting for me.

But not a soul was anywhere near our Maple.

I ran all the way to The Home, thankful the sidewalks were mostly dry except for crusty black snow along the edges. Banging the girls' door open, I rushed past the office. "Good afternoon, Miss Ritz. Sorry."

"Slow down, Debbie." Miss Ritz didn't look up from her typewriter.

In the dormitory, everyone was busy making the usual after-school racket, playing hand games, doing homework, or just chatting. Mrs. Petersen headed for her radio as I sailed by and called out, "Good afternoon, Mrs. Petersen."

Beverly lay on her bed reading a book or at least pretending to. Mary Ellen's bed was empty. I tossed my books and coat in the Big Girls' Room and sprinted into the washroom.

There stood Mary Ellen at a sink holding the back of her hand under a stream of water. Bright red blood swirled down the drain.

"Oh, my goodness." I wrapped my arms around her. "What happened?"

"I—I—got cut—" Her voice trailed off into a sob.

Snatching a long strip of toilet paper, I turned off the water and quickly pressed the paper to the back of Mary Ellen's hand. "Come with me."

I led her down the aisle like we had nothing important to do. The only girl paying any attention to us was Beverly who barely turned her head. But I saw her squinty eyes watching us like a hawk. Keeping the paper pressed tightly to Mary Ellen's hand, I pulled her along.

Thank you, Lord, I prayed, because Mrs. Petersen was busy finding her radio station. And Miss Ritz's office door was open, but she wasn't in there. Somehow, we made it all the way to the infirmary with no one noticing. I was getting too good at sneaking around.

Without a sound I closed the door and sat Mary Ellen on the edge of a bed. I pulled her into a tight hug. My sweet almost-sister sobbed and sobbed. "I didn't mean to," she said over and over between gasping breaths.

"It's all right," I said. "It's all right."

When Mary Ellen slowed down to just sucking in air and letting it out in shaky breaths, I went and tugged a chair over to a white cabinet high on the wall and found a roll of gauze, some adhesive tape, and Mercurochrome.

"I know you didn't mean to cut yourself." I sat next to Mary Ellen. "How did it happen?"

"I can't tell you." Mary Ellen hiccupped. "She'll make me sorry."

My mouth got so hard I couldn't get a single word out. How dare she threaten my Mary Ellen. "Did Beverly have something to do with this?" My words came out in a growl.

Mary Ellen's eyes got big and round.

Forcing a softer tone, I went on, "I won't tell her you told me. What happened?"

Mary Ellen hesitated for only a moment, which made my chest get tight knowing she trusted me that much.

"I told her I was waiting for you, but she wouldn't go away." Another hiccup. "When you didn't come, she told me they took you to the hospital, and I had to go with her. But she didn't go the right way. She went in the alley!"

I shot a loud breath out of my nose.

Mary Ellen's eyes got big and shiny.

"Don't worry, I'm not mad at you," I said. "Go on, tell me what happened."

"She said if I'd be her blood brother, she would have to be nice to me. She said no one else could be it."

"What are you talking about?"

"Blood brothers, you know like Jeff and Porky did."

That's when I knew this was worse than I'd thought. If Mrs. Petersen or Miss Ritz found out what happened, none of us would get to watch any television at all anymore. As it was, the only show we were allowed was Lassie on Sunday nights. And yesterday, the show had Jeff and his best friend Porky making themselves blood brothers. Of course, Lassie had tried to stop them from using a pocket knife to nick their thumbs and press them together mixing up their blood, but Mary Ellen had fallen asleep by then.

"Where did Beverly get a pocket knife?"

"She didn't use one. She found a big piece of green glass."

"You mean part of a pop bottle?"

"Uh-huh. I didn't want a cut on my thumb, because you know . . . "

"That's none of her business." I didn't need to see the callous right below Mary Ellen's knuckle, to remember she got it from sucking her thumb.

"She didn't care what I wanted. She made a little tiny cut on her thumb and squeezed out a dot of blood, but I couldn't do it. She grabbed the glass from me and squeezed my thumb so tight, I was scared. When I tried to pull my hand away from her, the glass cut the back of my hand."

Mary Ellen looked like she was ready to start crying all over again.

"It's okay. What did she do then?"

"She said I was too little to be a blood brother and ran away. I tried to follow her, but she went too fast."

"How'd you get back?"

"Paul found me. He told me not to tell anyone," Mary Ellen said. "He said I needed to wash it really good."

The door swung open.

I gasped.

Mary Ellen shouted, "Paul!"

"Sh-h-h-h." Paul and I shushed Mary Ellen at the same time.

"I thought I'd find you here," Paul said closing the door lickety-split. "That cut looked pretty bad."

Between the two of us we managed to get the wound bandaged. Paul held Mary Ellen's hand ever so gently and told her it would sting for only a minute. I dipped the glass stick into the small bottle of Mercurochrome and let it drip onto the cut. When it wouldn't stop bleeding, Paul knew exactly how to pull the skin together with short strips of adhesive tape.

"You are a very brave little girl," Paul said.

Mary Ellen beamed.

"Now you need to be a very tricky little girl," I said. "You don't want to let that mean girl know how much she hurt you because that will probably make her worse. You've got to make sure no one sees this bandage."

Hiding her hand behind her back, Mary Ellen grinned at Paul.

He peeked around her. "Uh-oh, I see it."

With her eyebrows all scrunched up she folded her arms and tried to hide her hand in the crook of her elbow. When Paul made a fake scared face because he could see it, she slid her hand along her side in-between the folds of the skirt on her dress. "Look, now no one can see it!"

"You're tricky and smart!" Paul winked at me over Mary Ellen's head.

"Thanks, Paul," I said. "We'd better get back."

He opened the door checking the hall. "All's clear."

I guided Mary Ellen back to the dormitory. Listening at the door, I cracked it open to peek inside. Everyone was still busy. I hustled to the Big Girls' Room. Mary Ellen followed stopping at her bed. Looking very natural, she slid her hand under her pillow and opened the book she'd left next to it.

I didn't miss the haughty smile on Beverly's face. Like she thought, she could get away with anything and was above everyone else like royalty. I ignored "Her Highness." It was a mean name to think up for a new girl, but it suited her perfectly. I knew Gram would be disappointed in me for thinking it up, but I couldn't help myself. And, mostly, I knew I couldn't do anything about the way she acted, so I decided right then and there to ignore Beverly. And, my conscience.

CHAPTER FIFTEEN

UNCHARITABLE

Watching out for Mary Ellen turned out to be almost a full-time job. Especially with her bed right next to Her Highness. Every night, before Mrs. Petersen announced ten minutes until lights out for the dormitory, I kept the Big Girls' Room door open a crack. Mary Ellen waited till Beverly went to the washroom before she put on pajamas and hung her dress on the hook next to her bed, exactly like I had told her. After Mary Ellen used the washroom, she kept her back to Beverly and got under her covers before Mrs. Petersen even turned out the lights.

Beverly kept up her constant complaining until none of the girls wanted anything to do with her. But at least Noreen had stopped sleeping the whole time after school. I could tell she was still sad, but now she did homework or prayed her rosary until Mrs. Petersen rang her bell for supper.

On Saturday before lunch, Eileen held the dormitory door open with her shoulder and called out, "Laundry's here." She balanced two full baskets, one on top of the other, to let Patricia come in.

Patricia set her load inside the door. She took a corrugated box off the top of another basket of laundry. "But, first, we have this," she said smiling. Setting the box in the aisle, she stepped back. The way she watched all of us girls jump up and rush over to the box, I bet she remembered the wonderful feeling of hoping the perfect dress had arrived just for her.

Mrs. Petersen dragged her rocking chair to the dormitory aisle. "Before you girls find your unmentionables and choose your dress for this week, let's take a look at these things from the Missionary Aid Society." She set her chair right next to the box, sat down, and opened it.

Excited, I pressed closer like everyone else. Everyone, that is, except Her Highness who lay on her bed with a book. It seemed like that was all she was ever going to do.

Pulling out the clothes one by one, Mrs. Petersen set a white blouse with tiny flowers on her lap and held up the small jumper that went with it. Red corduroy.

"That's beautiful!" Mary Ellen said. She used her left hand to tug on my slacks, keeping her right in the folds of her skirt. "It's almost like the one you get sometimes."

"Come here then, turn around, and let's see if it's your size." Mrs. Petersen held the jumper up to Mary Ellen's shoulders. Looking up she said, "It's a wee bit long. Patricia, could you hem it?"

"Yes, ma'am. About two inches?"

Nodding, Mrs. Petersen pulled out another dress. "Isn't this pink gingham lovely," she said.

The dress had a little cape attached over the shoulders with a scalloped edge that hung over the bodice. It was interesting like whoever wore it would be saying something out of the ordinary about themselves, but I wasn't sure what.

"That is the ugliest dress I've ever seen," Beverly declared loudly before anyone else had a chance to comment. "It looks like it should be hanging from someone's curtain rods."

She was paying attention after all.

"It's not that bad. Turn around dear," Mrs. Petersen said to Diane who stood next to her chair. "Humph. Too big." She scanned the rest of the girls, her eyes settling on me. "Might fit you. Come here and let's see."

"No." I said way too loudly. "Thank you, but I already have plenty of dresses to choose from every week."

"Do you now?" Mrs. Petersen held the dress up and studied it. I saw her peek at Beverly.

"Eileen, could you remove this cape?"

Eileen mumbled a "yes, ma'am," and took the dress. Everyone knew she could barely sew a hem. I was pretty sure Mrs. Petersen was saving all of us from that dress and especially Beverly's opinion.

Under the now-awful pink gingham was a stack of dingy underpants. "Humph. Eileen, please take care of these, too." Even Miss Ritz believed a girl should not have to wear hand-me-down underwear, thank goodness.

There were several pairs of slacks and blouses the girls could wear on Saturdays and some socks in pretty good shape. The last was a dress with a dark turquoise blue bodice in a shiny fabric and a striped skirt with the same blue, plus black and red. It was beautiful. All the girls murmured complimentary comments, except for Her Highness, of course. I saw her peek at the dress and turn back to her book. I guessed if she couldn't say something mean she wouldn't say anything at all.

Again, Mrs. Petersen looked over the group of girls passing over me with a little frown of regret. "Nancy, you're getting big. Let's see if this will do for you this week."

Trying to swallow my disappointment, I turned to Mary Ellen. "That red jumper is perfect for you with your dark hair and blue eyes."

"I love it," Mary Ellen said. "Pick the blue jumper this week so we can look like sisters."

Mary Ellen's excitement almost made me forget my disappointment until Beverly piped up with, "Jumpers are for babies. I haven't worn one since kindergarten."

"What do you know?" Sharon hurried to stick up for me. "All the high school girls wear them."

"Certainly not corduroy!" Her Highness said acting shocked.

"Girls, girls, no bickering." Mrs. Petersen got up from her chair. She picked up a basket of clean clothes and set it on the end of Beverly's bed. Then she headed into the Big Girls' Room with another basket which was not something she usually did. I wondered if she needed to get away for a moment.

Two girls began going through the clean clothes in the basket on Beverly's bed causing some pretty, lavender underpants to land on her leg. She snatched them up. "These are mine. Why are they mixed in with all of that?" Her nose wrinkled in disgust.

"Listen, missy," Eileen growled in a low voice. "You'd best be opening them ears of yours. Mrs. Petersen already told you them baskets is all the girls' laundry. You can stop being so high and mighty and be glad you're not the one doing it." She picked up the basket. Turning her back to Her Highness with a haughty attitude of her own, she set it on the next bed.

As if she hadn't heard one word from Eileen, Beverly began to fold her underpants. "What in the world is this?" Her voice could surely be heard all the way across the street to the Solomon's house. "Someone wrote on my underwear!" She held up the offending item with the *B. Jensen* clearly visible.

Eileen whipped around and snatched the underpants out of every-one's view. "What is wrong with you holding up personal items for all the world to see?" She slapped them onto Beverly's bed scowling. "Everyone's undergarments are marked. How else could we tell them apart?"

Mrs. Petersen came back into the dormitory. Acting like she hadn't heard a thing, she spoke directly to Her Highness, "Every Saturday each girl picks out a dress for the week."

"One dress for a whole week is ridiculous." Beverly stood up and put her hands on her hips. "Wait, what do you mean, picks out? Where are my clothes?" she demanded.

"It seems you have not been listening very well." Mrs. Petersen spoke very slowly. "As I said, all the girls' laundry is done together. Surely you can understand we cannot have some girls with more or better clothing than others. Now, there are three baskets. Patricia and Eileen separate the clothing by size. Your underwear should be in this basket and you may choose one dress," she said. "Just one."

Beverly didn't move except to thrust her chin out and scowl.

Why did Mrs. Petersen put up with that girl's behavior? If anyone else carried on like that, Miss Ritz would be called on to straighten her out for sure. But Mrs. Petersen just turned and began pulling her chair back into her room.

"Let's get out of here," Sharon said.

Noreen led the way and the three of us headed for the Big Girls' Room. As I passed Mary Ellen's bed, the little girl climbed onto it and stood in the middle while Patricia pulled the red jumper over her head. "You don't need the blouse on for me to do this."

"But, it's so pretty."

"Let me hem the jumper and then you can try them both on."

Mary Ellen pushed her right arm into the jumper.

"And, what is this?" Patricia touched the bandage.

Jerking her hand behind her back, Mary Ellen said, "Nothing, really, it's nothing."

Patricia noticed me watching and lifted her eyebrows, but then she turned away. "Hold still then, I don't want to poke you."

I scooted into the Big Girls' Room.

"That new girl is . . ." Sharon paused closing the door. "I don't know what to call her. She's unbelievable!"

"She's just plain mean." I thought of Mary Ellen's bandaged hand, but I couldn't talk about it, not even to Sharon and Noreen.

Gram always said if you tell a secret to only one person you might as well tell a dozen because it would be only a matter of time until the whole world knew. I'd already told Sharon one secret, so I certainly wasn't going to tell her anything about my little sis. If Mary Ellen's story got out, I was sure no one would get to watch television for a long time. That would be so unfair to everyone. Besides, Mary Ellen would have to share the blame for it, and I couldn't let that happen.

"And selfish," Sharon said.

"Don't be so quick to judge," Noreen said.

"I'm not judging," Sharon argued. "It's as plain as the nose on your face, don't ya know. She's awful. Anyone can see that. Someone needs to put the kibosh on her and be quick about it."

I stayed out of it, mostly I was thankful that Noreen was feeling good enough to argue her point. But I knew something was going on with Beverly because it looked like she wasn't getting a haircut like the rest of us anytime soon.

"There must be more to her story than we can even imagine. It's not like Mrs. Petersen to let a girl talk to her like that." Noreen always thought the best of everyone.

"As if we don't all have a sad story," Sharon said.

Noreen picked up her rosary and sat on the edge of her bed. "I think we should pray for her."

CHAPTER SIXTEEN

UNKNOWN

A knock at the door of the Big Girls' Room interrupted our "Beverly" discussion.

Mrs. Petersen peeked in. "We are having a bit of outdoor time before lunch. The sun is bright. A little fresh air will do everyone some good." Glancing at Noreen, she added, "I've said it's mandatory, but, if you want to stay here, my dear, watch the clock. Lunch is at the regular time in thirty-five minutes."

"I'm going." I grabbed my coat from its hook. I couldn't let Mary Ellen be stuck in the play yard with Beverly.

"Go ahead." Sharon reached for her own coat. To Noreen she said, "Some fresh air is a good idea. Come along Noreen. I'll wait for you."

In the dormitory, Mary Ellen stood in the aisle with her back to the row of beds, trying to button her coat with one hand. Squatting down, I did it for her and took her good hand in mine.

"Let's hurry before all the swings are taken," I said.

The play yard looked inviting with the sun shining brightly. Usually the boys and girls had separate turns in the yard, but, sometimes, when we had a short time to play, we were together. The housemothers each sat in chairs near the gate keeping a sharp eye out for any wrong behavior.

I let go of Mary Ellen's hand right inside the gate. She passed some girls drawing a hopscotch on the concrete near the building. Running across the gravel, she got the last swing. As soon as she sat on the board seat, it looked like she realized she couldn't swing with only one hand.

Beverly stepped in front of her with her arms across her chest. Didn't she know it was dangerous to stand in the way of the swings? I couldn't tell if Her Highness said anything, but Mary Ellen jumped off the swing and skipped over to the hopscotchers.

The boys swarmed through the gate. A quick tug on my coat sleeve startled me. Paul breezed past. What did he want? I watched him pick up a rolling ball and toss it back to a trio of younger boys playing catch. Then he darted behind the brick chimney that went all the way up the side of the building to the roof. I grinned. All Miss Nielsen could see of him were the tips of his shoes.

Heading to join Paul, I stopped to watch Mary Ellen jump into each numbered square for hopscotch.

"You're out. You stepped over the line," a third-grade girl called out.

"She was on the line," I said. "That always counts for first graders." I gave the girl a don't-be-so-hard-on-her look. Just like a big sister should. "I was watching. She was very close, but not over it."

Glancing over my shoulder, I made sure our housemothers weren't looking my way. I slipped around the chimney and pressed my back against the brick wall. I checked the toes of my shoes to make sure they did not stick out like Paul's.

"I never noticed what big feet you have," I said. A big brother should have big feet.

"That's a fine greeting for someone who managed to get these." Paul held out three Band-Aids.

"Where did you ever get them? They're perfect."

"I can't tell," he said wiggling his eyebrows.

I slipped them into my coat pocket

"Has anyone said anything about her bandage?" Paul asked.

"Patricia saw it this morning," I said. "But, when Mary Ellen told her it was nothing, Patricia let it go. I don't think anyone else noticed or cared to ask about it. Most of the girls have been here long enough to know how things go."

"No one wants to get anyone else in trouble," Paul said.

"Except maybe Her Highness," I said lifting my chin toward the swings.

"Her Highness, ha," Paul said. "That's exactly what she thinks. But, she's probably afraid she'll get in trouble, too."

"I don't think she's afraid of anything."

I watched Beverly glide back and forth on the swing. She didn't go particularly high, yet she seemed to float through the air. Her pumping motions were so graceful a girl couldn't help but notice.

"I heard some things from a boy at school," Paul said.

"Really?" I was amazed even high school kids knew of her.

"He told me his cousin used to live down the block from a family in Lincoln Park that I'm pretty sure was Beverly's."

Everyone knew all the rich and mighty folks lived in Lincoln Park. "That figures," I said. "But what makes you think he was talking about Beverly's family?"

"He said the only survivor of a family was sent to a children's home, so he was asking if we had a new girl. Anyway, he said, in this family, the mother died when their only child, a girl, was born, and the father was some kinda big shot who got it somehow." Paul drew his finger across his neck. "Maybe from the mob."

I gasped.

"He also said the girl's the one who found him, but I don't know if I believe that part."

"I don't know how anyone could stand that," I said. "Maybe Mrs. Petersen knows and that's why she lets her behave the way she does."

"Maybe. But just because something bad happens doesn't give a person any excuses in my book." Paul turned his face away.

I could still hear his swallow.

"It does make me feel awfully sorry for her," I said.

"That's because you're nice. Unlike her. Anyway, another kid at school claimed her father, you know," Paul tipped his hand up to his mouth like someone drinking, "killed himself with too much of it."

My knees started shaking. I carefully lowered my eyes. I couldn't look at Paul. What if he knew about my mother? What would he think? But he didn't seem to notice my reaction and went right on talking.

"I think the first story is nearer the truth. From the look of her and her attitude, she doesn't seem like someone who'd have a drunkard for a father."

Heat rushed to my cheeks.

A whistle blast shrilled through the air letting all of us know it was time to leave.

I couldn't let Paul see my face. I couldn't let him guess what I was thinking. "See you," I said pushing off the wall as fast as a bullet.

I hurried over and got first in the line. Mrs. Petersen held a basket for everyone who filed through the gate to place their balls and jump ropes and chalk. I nodded at her. Hustling up the stairs, I hurried to the Big Girls' Room to put my coat away. The Band-Aids fit right in the pocket of my slacks.

Mrs. Petersen rang her bell. "Lunch time."

I got in line behind Mary Ellen. She crossed her legs and bounced. "I need to go," she told Mrs. Petersen.

Looking frazzled, Mrs. Petersen stuttered, "Um, well . . . "

"I'll help her," I said.

"Thank you. But, do hurry."

"We will."

In the bathroom, Mary Ellen finished up, and I turned on one of the sinks.

"Don't get the back of your hand wet," I said. I pulled the red string on one of the Band-Aids. "Clear. That's even better," I said, when I saw what was inside the wax paper wrapper.

It took only a moment or two to replace Mary Ellen's bandage with one of the new ones. Putting it at an angle, only a tiny red line peeked out of one corner. "This should be much easier to hide," I said. "If it starts to get loose, tell me. Paul gave me three of these."

"All I see now is my hand. Thanks." Mary Ellen ran out the door and down the stairs with me close behind.

Feeling like such a good "big sister" I smiled to myself, but I couldn't get the stories about Beverly out of my thoughts. It would be awful for anyone to find their father like that boy said, but it would be worse if the other story were true. I knew that for sure. Could that really happen? Could a person drink themselves to death? I grabbed the banister to keep steady. That would be beyond awful.

No one would want anything to do with me if they knew the reason I was at The Home. Not even Paul, that was for sure.

CHAPTER SEVENTEEN

UNLOVED

"Let's go to the game room," Sharon said after lunch.

Noreen lay on her bed facing the wall. "I'll stay here," she said.

Yesterday, I'd thought Noreen was feeling better, but now she looked really sad again. Maybe with only the two of us, Noreen and I could talk about the fire and all. I didn't like to go to the game room anyway. But, when Sharon took off, she left the door open.

Stepping over to close it, I noticed both Mary Ellen and Beverly's beds were empty. They must be in the game room since it was the only place a girl could go right after lunch on a Saturday afternoon when it was cold outside. Now, I'd have to go, too. Maybe a good rest would be best for Noreen.

The game room was a place I had hated ever since my first day at The Home. That day I'd had to leave my favorite doll there. Then I'd had to endure watching other girls play with her as if she was any old doll. I didn't bring the doll to play with. I only wanted to keep her on my bed. I was only seven when Daddy gave me Elizabeth Anne because he had to go to Korea.

After that first day, I avoided the game room. Whenever I had to go there, I told myself that doll wasn't Elizabeth Anne. Not anymore. It wasn't so hard to believe once someone had changed her clothes.

After a while it got easier to forget how wonderful she was when the perfect pale blue ribbon in her hair got untied and then dirty and then lost. Now, it seemed like that had all happened a long time ago. Today, I'd focus on watching out for Mary Ellen.

"Who wants to play?" Sharon called out from a table near the door. She set the Monopoly board out and began sorting the real estate cards and separating the money. "I'll be the banker." As soon as she added that three girls joined her. No one ever wanted to be the banker.

I spotted Mary Ellen sitting on the floor near a white doll cradle with only part of one rocker broken off. No surprise, Beverly was heading over to her. I whisked past Her Highness and squatted down next to Mary Ellen. "So, what's your doll's name?"

"She's not mine," Mary Ellen said. "None of the dolls belong to anyone."

"I know," I said. "We have to share everything here."

Out of the corner of my eye I could see Beverly looking out the window.

"I still like to play with them." Mary Ellen's quiet voice made me forget Her Highness.

Mary Ellen smoothed the dark hair of a baby doll in red overalls. "This one is Kathleen Anne today," she said. "That's what I always call them."

"I had a doll named Elizabeth Anne once," I said. "Before I came here."

"Really? Mine was Kathleen Anne. And, I had a monkey called Bo-Bo."

I caught Mary Ellen's eyes before she looked down at the doll. I could tell she knew what it was like to love a doll and then have to let it go. Mary Ellen was so much like me.

Picking up a tall, blonde doll in a raggedy, pink dress, I held her by the legs and walked her over to the cradle. "It's time for bed, Kathleen Anne," I said in a sweetie-pie voice. "Come along now, I want to be a good babysitter so you must take a nap."

Mary Ellen walked the curved legs of the baby doll over to the cradle and hopped her into it. "Nighty, night, Kathleen Anne."

I smoothed a wrinkled blanket over the doll. "You take a nice nap now."

Mary Ellen giggled. "Would you play Pick-Up-Sticks with me?"

Nodding, I warned her, "I'm an ace at Pick-Up-Sticks."

"That's okay."

Holding hands, we went to find the game. We played it until Miss Nielsen arrived at the door. "Time's up, girls." She crossed her arms. Everyone hurried to put things away and get in line to go back to the dormitory until supper time.

Going up the stairs, Mary Ellen whispered, "I would have won that last game."

"You're right."

It seemed downright silly to me that no one could ever take anything out of the game room. Who would it hurt if we'd brought Pick-Up Sticks to the dorm and played it a little longer? Probably none of the boys would even take that game out of the cabinet when they had their turn in the game room until supper. The Home had so many rules. It wasn't fair.

For the next two hours, I went back and forth between the Big Girls' Room and the washroom. It was the best way to keep an eye on Mary Ellen. And Beverly. Her Highness spent the whole time pretending to sleep. More than once I saw her turn her head and peek under her eyelashes to spy on someone in the dormitory. One time she had the gall to do it to me. But I got her goat by stopping in my tracks. I folded my arms across my chest and stared right at her. Beverly wasn't fooling me one bit when she pretended to roll over in her sleep.

It seemed like forever, but Mrs. Petersen finally rang her little bell. We all headed down to supper. In the dining hall, I could relax since Mary Ellen and Beverly sat at different tables.

For once, I was glad we couldn't talk during meals. It gave me a chance to let my hopes and dreams dance all around in my thoughts. I was sure Miss Ritz's special outing would change my life forever. I was sure the couple who took me out would like me so much they'd want to adopt me because I planned to do everything I could to make them want me to be a part of their family. Who could resist polite and pleasant and friendly but not too talkative? Most of all, I'd tell them how I felt with my eyes.

Eating in silence had taught me exactly how to do that. Funny thing about talking with your eyes. That's how someone might say it, "she told me she liked my dress with her eyes." But really my eyebrows and my face would do the talking. Or, maybe how I opened my eyes wide, or squinted them, or winked. Truth was I was pretty sure I knew how to talk with my eyes better than anyone.

The next morning during church, Paul shouted out, "Amen," before the congregation finished saying, "But, deliver us from evil." Miss Nielsen had him by the ear in a split second. When he didn't show up in the front parlor after supper to watch *Lassie*, I could tell Noreen was really down in the dumps. I didn't blame her one bit. Paul was the best big brother ever, even to me and Mary Ellen.

After lights out in the dormitory, I read the last chapter of *Gone Away Lake*. Portia and Blake ended up living happily ever after. Their family planned to get a vacation home on the lake. I reread the last page twice, because that's always my favorite. The end was when everything turned out okay after all no matter how much it had seemed like it wouldn't. The second time through I heard Sharon's snoring, maybe Noreen would talk now.

So, I called her name in the dark. "Noreen? Are you awake?"

"Just a little."

"Did you get to see Paul after church today?" I asked.

"No."

"I think your brother Paul standing up for what he believes is a fine thing."

"I wish he wouldn't shout like that in church."

Holding my breath, I waited.

"But it is the first time he cared enough to do that since . . . " Noreen's voice faded away.

I was more patient than I'd ever thought I could be.

Finally, Noreen went on, "At first, I couldn't think of anything else."

"Uh-huh." My response was soft so Noreen would know I was listening.

"Then I was afraid the—fire—and what happened to my parents meant God didn't love me anymore."

I tiptoed over to Noreen and, kneeling beside her, lay my hand on her cheek. I gently wiped away a tear. I thought of seeing Gram read her Bible every day so I was sure she knew a lot about God. And she always said, "God's love is perfect. It doesn't depend on what we do."

"I just know God loves you," I whispered. Praying silently, I asked God, *Please make her know You love her.*

Moments passed. Noreen took a shaky breath, but her cheek stayed dry. I let my hand slide down to the edge of her bed.

"On the way to church today," Noreen said. "Paul and I were talking about our friends that are gone. One girl, Janice Baker, got to be my best friend the year before we graduated eighth-grade, but she went to a different high school. I've been wondering if she knows."

I nodded in the dark, as if she could see me.

"I'm glad Paul shouted out, 'Amen', like he used to. And, today, I listened to everyone else recite the part he refuses to say. Really for the first time."

"For thine is the kingdom, and the power, and the glory, forever and ever," I said.

"That's it. And, I think," Noreen talked slowly like she was choosing each word carefully. "Well, actually, I know, that's all true, too."

I was so glad she knew that. "I remember the first time I heard Paul shout, 'Amen'. When you told me why, I knew God liked it. No one should say things they don't believe."

"Really? But, you're not Catholic."

"My Gram taught me to believe what's in the Bible," I said. "That's more important than what any church says."

"I suppose that's not a bad idea." Noreen sounded interested in talking, which was way better than she'd been. "We believe it's important to be baptized Catholic. That's how you can get into heaven. That's why I can't stop thinking about—everyone I knew."

I was sure most of the students at Our Lady, and Noreen and Paul's parents, must have been baptized Catholic. So, I thought through what

I wanted to say next and tried to say it carefully. "Saying you have to be Catholic to go to heaven, well, that's not in the Bible. Neither is any other religion I've ever heard of. I looked. The Bible says Jesus is the only way to heaven and that's what I believe."

Noreen took a long time to answer. So long, I worried I made things worse for her.

But then Noreen's voice marched into the dark room, quiet but strong. "If the Catholic church is wrong," she said sounding almost like her old self, "then I'm sure the Pope will figure it out and make sure all of us know. That's his job."

I didn't answer because what she said made a lot of sense. Besides, I didn't want to argue, especially when Noreen sounded so confident and powerful. Smiling in the dark, I patted her arm and tiptoed back to bed. After a few minutes I started breathing slowly and evenly to make Noreen think I was asleep. Tomorrow night, I'd have to ask Noreen to tell me how she prayed with her rosary. That would be good for her, too.

CHAPTER EIGHTEEN

UNWANTED

Monday morning, on the way out of the girl's door, I whispered to Mary Ellen, "I forgot my homework. I'll catch up to you in a minute." Darting back up the stairs and past Mrs. Petersen, I grinned. Using my happy-go-lucky voice, I said, "Silly me. Forgot my homework."

Mrs. Petersen frowned. But, thankfully, she did not ask for an explanation.

How could I explain? Instead of paying attention to what I was doing I'd been thinking of how I'd smile and what I'd say to my family at the outing. I'd pulled on my coat, grabbed Mary Ellen's hand, and left without my school things. It was as simple as that, but I was pretty sure Mrs. Petersen would call it daydreaming, not concentrating.

Passing by her again at the top of the stairs I said, "Have a nice day."

That surprised her so much, she didn't ask any questions at all, she just mumbled thanks.

Opening the girls' door for a second time, I spotted Mary Ellen standing on the sidewalk in front of The Home. Tears ran down her cheeks. I didn't miss the fact that Her Highness was turning the corner toward school.

"What's the matter?" I crouched down in front of my almost-sister.

"Are . . . " Mary Ellen pressed her fists to her eyes.

Letting my books slide onto the sidewalk, I pulled her into a hug. "It's okay. It's okay."

Mary Ellen took in a shaky breath. "Are we . . . " Her words came out hot against my neck. "Are—we unwanted?"

"Unwanted?" What a question. How could I answer? I patted Mary Ellen's back. "No," I said even though I wasn't sure. "Of course not. What would make you ask such a thing?"

"But—she said . . . " Mary Ellen hiccupped and squeezed my neck. Then she let go and pointed at the words chiseled into the stone over the front door.

"What do you mean?" I read the words aloud, "That says 'The Evergreen Home for Children in Need.'"

"That's not what she said. Beverly told me it says, 'For Unwanted Children'." Mary Ellen scowled at the letters. She wiped the tears off her face, put her hands on her hips, and added, "She's so mean."

"She is." I loved Mary Ellen's spunk. "So, let's just ignore her. Besides, if The Home was for unwanted children, and she lives here too, that would make her unwanted, wouldn't it?"

Mary Ellen laughed, every trace of her tears gone.

"We'd better hurry now."

"Let's go." Mary Ellen started off skipping toward school.

Following at a quick pace, my thoughts ran all over willy-nilly. I had to do something to protect Mary Ellen from that girl. When the school building loomed ahead, we slowed down. "And I will, too," I said aloud. "Even if it's the last thing I do."

"What did you say?" Mary Ellen asked.

"Um, ah." Did I say that out loud? "Can you walk home without me after school today?"

"Sure." Mary Ellen skipped off to the other first-graders by the side entrance.

Amazed at how quickly Mary Ellen had forgotten her tears and trauma, I squinted my eyes looking for Her Highness. I finally spotted her red coat right in the middle of a group of fifth grade girls who looked like they were hanging on her every word.

"What are you fuming over?"

I answered Doris without taking my eyes off Beverly, "Actually, it's *who*."

"Oh, her," Doris said. "What's she up to now?"

"You won't believe it." Telling Doris how that mean, snotty girl made Mary Ellen cry fired up my determination. "I've got to figure out how to stop her."

"But, how?" Doris said.

"I've got all day to figure that out." I scowled. "But, I will."

Even with my thoughts awhirl, I managed to follow all Mr. Kelly's directions and stay out of trouble all day. And, amazingly, he got his film ready to roll in record time.

"Today's film," Mr. Kelly said, "*It's Our War, Too!*, explains the role women played in World War II."

Throwing a giggly glance over her shoulder, Doris made a burst of laughter flare up in my throat. But I slapped my hand over my mouth just in time.

After Mr. Kelly went on and on telling us all the important contributions women made during the war, it seemed to me like there was no point in showing the film. While the clickety film rolled, I decided I would have to tell Her Highness to knock it off and leave Mary Ellen alone. If I stood firm like Miss Nielsen did when she reprimanded one of the big boys, all tough and mean looming over them, maybe I'd scare Beverly into stopping. It seemed like the only choice.

My mind made up, I watched the women in uniform marching along in front of the blackboard. I thought I'd been ignoring everything Mr. Kelly had said before starting the film, when his words came drifting into my head. "During the war, women became more confident." That was it! Today, after school, I'd stand up to Her Highness all right, but not mean like Miss Nielsen. I would handle her like a confident woman would. A strong, confident woman like Miss Ritz or Gram.

As soon as Mr. Kelly said, "You are dismissed," I jumped up from my seat and got in line before most of the others. Darting into the hall, I went the opposite direction toward the fifth-grade classrooms. When Beverly came out of her room with several girls surrounding her, I pretended to tie my shoe until they paraded by.

Keeping a bit of distance, I followed them until they reached the corner at Holman. Beverly paused and with her nose in the air said, "Tomorrow then." The girls sighed and drifted off in twos and threes while I closed the gap.

"Hi, Beverly," I said with my own nose a bit higher than usual.

Her Highness squinted. "What do you want?" Her voice was low as if she didn't want to be overheard by her classmates.

"We need to talk."

Beverly eyes narrowed, and she lifted her chin. "I don't."

I almost faltered, but Gram's words encouraged me, "You catch more flies with honey than vinegar."

"I know you're new at The Home." I used a confident voice, kind but firm. "Which is why you don't understand how things are."

Not backing down a bit, Her Highness responded, "I understand everything."

"No. You do not."

"I knew right from the start how to keep you in line. You care more for that silly little baby than you care about yourself."

"What?" Beverly had picked on Mary Ellen and even hurt her just to get at me?

A satisfied grin started to spread across Beverly's face.

Anger swelled in me. "That's not the way we behave here. That's not the way anyone should behave anywhere."

Beverly shrugged.

I stepped right up to her with my head held high. "At The Home we treat each other with kindness. And, we don't hurt each other. Especially the little ones. Especially Mary Ellen. I expect you to stay away from her."

Beverly glared up at me. I glared right back staring straight into her eyes. We stood like that for what seemed like forever—each of us trying to stare down the other. When Beverly's left eyelid started to twitch, I realized I didn't feel like blinking at all, and we both knew if Beverly did blink, I won.

Beverly could tell I wasn't going to blink. Ever.

"You don't scare me," she said not moving an inch.

"I'm not trying to scare you," I said. "I'm teaching you to behave."

"You're teaching me?" Beverly's jaw clenched, and her eyelid stopped twitching.

But I knew I was right, and she was wrong. Just knowing that made me stare without any meanness at all. I knew my stare was righteous.

Beverly must have known too because I saw a glint of fear seeping into her eyes. A moment later, Beverly turned away her shoulders slumping and mumbled, "Fine."

"Thank you," I said pleasantly as if I'd been handed a treat and planned to share it.

Before I could move, Beverly pulled her shoulders up and marched off, her blonde braids bouncing and still longer than any other girls at The Home. I knew I had handled the whole situation perfectly. Thanks to Gram, which was not surprising, and a WWII film, which was a huge surprise. But, the biggest shock of all was the fact that I had to give at least a little credit to Mr. Kelly.

Beverly had seemed defeated, but would she do what I'd said? Even Her Highness must know the stare down rule, "Never mess with the winner again." I knew one thing for sure. There was no way she would make it back to the dormitory in time, but that was her problem.

It wasn't my fault Her Highness had marched off in the wrong direction.

CHAPTER NINETEEN

UNTHINKABLE

Sure enough, Beverly got back to The Home almost a half hour late. When she strolled in, Mrs. Petersen did not look up from the arithmetic book she held with Nancy at her elbow. She did not pick up her watch from her bosom or act like the late arrival was a problem at all. Even Mrs. Petersen treated Beverly like she was Her Highness.

Standing in the doorway of the Big Girls' Room, I made eye contact with Beverly. She looked away quickly and then sat on her bed with her back to Mary Ellen. Maybe she didn't quite feel like Her Highness anymore, and maybe she would stop being so mean. At least to Mary Ellen.

Closing the door, I started in on my homework. A few minutes later, Noreen and Sharon got back from school and did homework, too, until Mrs. Petersen rang her bell for supper. In the dining hall, Paul gave his sister a smile and then winked at me. It made me smile until I remembered that Uncle Lloyd used to wink at me. I couldn't think of him and home and all that, so I decided to think up a daydream about the outing.

For the rest of the week, I walked Mary Ellen to and from school every day with no problems. Everyone was in a Christmassy mood including Mr. Kelly. I never did get a chance to tell him I was concentrating not daydreaming, but I also didn't have to write any sentences. Friday was our last day of school before two whole weeks of Christmas break.

At The Home, no one would call the mood Christmassy. By silent agreement, none of us girls talked about the Christmas traditions we remembered, but I still thought of all Gram taught me that Christmas meant. That filled a lot of the empty space in me. Besides, I could still look forward to the Sunday after Valentine's Day when I was sure to have a new family and scads of new Christmas traditions.

Late in the afternoon on Christmas Eve, Mrs. Petersen's bell rang out much longer and louder than usual. Sharon looked up from her paperback, "Holy-moly, who's making the racket?" She jumped up and opened our door. Noreen and I hurried to see, too.

Standing in the middle of the dormitory, Mrs. Petersen continued ringing her bell like she thought she was Santa himself. "Girls," she said with a huge smile on her face, "Our Christmas tree has arrived, and it's all trimmed. Tidy up now." She picked up her watch. "In ten minutes, we will all go down to the front parlor for a viewing." Letting her watch drop to her bosom, she went back to her room.

Sharon flopped back on her bed. "Why don't we get to decorate the tree?"

"Just imagine, all of us and one tree," Noreen said. "That would be topsy-turvy for sure."

Noreen seemed to be getting back to her old self. Back to being the peacemaker and trying to use silly words like Sharon always did.

I was going to say "Noreen's right. This isn't her first Christmas here," but I couldn't get the words out. Gram had ornaments from when she was a little girl, and, while we decorated the tree together, she told me the story for each one.

"Who does it?" Sharon asked.

"I think Mrs. Bell is in charge of it," Noreen said. "Patricia and Eileen must be the ones who get to decorate the tree."

By the time we got to the parlor I'd managed to push all my feelings out of my brain. The tall tree made all of us girls gasp at the same time. With its big colored lights, shiny ornaments, and individual strands of tinsel hanging from the tips of each branch, the tree was gorgeous.

The two overstuffed davenports and the heavy round coffee table had been removed from the parlor. The big television cabinet with its little black and white screen had been pushed to the other end. The tree, in all its glory, stood right in the middle of the room.

All my feelings—not being home for Christmas, Gram being gone, my whole family gone—gathered in my chest making it tight. So tight, I thought I'd die right then and there. Tears made my eyes blur. I concentrated on the real reason for Christmas praying God would help me bear it. Lots of girls sniffed and rubbed their arms over their eyes. Somehow knowing just about everyone else was struggling too made my breath go back to normal.

Mrs. Petersen took Beverly's hand in one of hers and Mary Ellen's in the other. I took hold of Mary Ellen's other hand and Noreen's. Around the tree, the other girls did the same until we had encircled the tree with outstretched arms. Mrs. Petersen started humming "Joy to the World." Still praying, I sang out the words, and everyone joined in. Before we finished the first song, the boys came down their stairs and, taking up the singing, joined our circle.

Paul took Noreen's other hand. Miss Nielsen was nowhere around, and it was a good thing because she would never tolerate girls and boys holding hands even though anywhere else no one would think it was wrong at all. Patricia got in between two boys who were leaving a space making it clear they didn't want to hold hands. Eileen stood leaning against the wall with her arms crossed and an almost happy look on her grumpy face.

Someone else started "Silent Night." I closed my eyes and sang out with real joy in my heart. "All is calm—"

The front door burst open with a crash.

I kept right on singing, "All is bright."

But, a lot of kids stopped. So, I opened my eyes to stare toward the noise at the door like everyone else. A dark-haired woman stood brushing snow off the shoulders of her green coat, but erratic strokes didn't seem to get the snow off the fur collar.

Miss Ritz rushed out of her office. She stood in front of the woman, her wide padded shoulders making it impossible for me to see the woman's face. "May I help you?"

"Round yon virgin," I sang. All alone. Everyone else had stopped. They all dropped hands and stopped where they were. Singing the next words, "mother and child," I took a few extra steps. With a clear view to the doorway, I stopped singing. And breathing.

The woman's voice rose blocking out all my thoughts and making my Christmas joy disappear like the snow on her collar as if she couldn't stand having it in the room. Or in my heart.

"I want to shh-ee my daww-ter," she said. The woman's voice slurred, but I still recognized it. Maybe that was why I recognized it. Since it had been the only voice I'd heard from her before Uncle Lloyd dumped me at The Home.

The woman was my mother.

CHAPTER TWENTY

UNFORGIVABLE

My mother's voice grew louder, "It's Chrisss-musss Eve and . . . "

For weeks I'd cried myself to sleep. I'd hoped and prayed and waited. She never came to see me. Not once. Not even when I had the mumps. After that, I had stopped thinking of her. I'd made myself stop, and, now, I never did and didn't want to start.

"I have a right to shh-ee my own daww-ter."

Sure. Seeing me was so important to her. Except for the first five months and five days I'd been here. If only the floor would open up and swallow me. This couldn't be happening. Not now. Not in front of everyone.

"Please step into my office." Miss Ritz held the woman's elbow and moved in that direction.

"Let me shh-ee my daww-ter." My mother jerked away, stumbled, and fell against the wall.

"Eileen, go to my file cabinet and look in the second drawer for the Spencer file." Miss Ritz led my mother toward her office. "Patricia. May I have your assistance?"

As Patricia took over for her, Miss Ritz turned to the tree and all of us. "Mrs. Petersen, I was enjoying your impromptu concert. Please continue."

Awkwardly, all of us joined hands around the tree starting with Mrs. Petersen claiming Mary Ellen and Beverly's. Mary Ellen picked up my hand. I let my other one hang at my side, but Noreen gently picked it up. Her warm fingers gave mine a tiny squeeze. Even though she'd heard Miss Ritz ask for the Spencer file. My file. Just like everyone heard. She squeezed anyway.

The singing began slowly, faltering.

"Deck the halls with boughs of holly."

By the time we got to the first *fa, la, las* it seemed almost normal. Almost happy. Except that my voice would not leave my throat, so I mouthed the words and pasted a smile on my face staring at the tree. And, only the tree.

Patricia's voice tickled my ear. "Miss Ritz wants you."

Without looking at anyone, I dropped Mary Ellen and Noreen's hands and followed Patricia, but I'd felt Noreen's quick squeeze before she let go. And that squeeze gave me enough courage to walk away from all the other girls and boys holding hands and singing around the Christmas tree.

Patricia led me into the office and closed the door behind me. My mother stood next to Miss Ritz and her desk.

"Thisss isss my daww-ter." My mother's voice was loud but might not be heard over the singing. She wrapped her arms around me and clung to me like she needed me, if only to stay upright. I wanted to step aside and watch her fall. I wanted to pay her back for all the times I'd longed to be needed and wanted but never was.

I pulled away from her arms.

She gave me a bleary-eyed gaze squinting like she couldn't see clearly. "Ssstill looksss jusss like her Daddy." And, with that, she crumpled backward. Miss Ritz scooted a chair behind her just in time.

Why was she here? Why now, after staying away forever?

After acting like I was as dead as Daddy?

Miss Ritz went around the desk to her chair as if my mother wasn't there bent over and crying into her lap. Smiling pleasantly at me, Miss Ritz said, "I've telephoned your Uncle Lloyd. He should be here in a little while."

I stood stock-still. His name made the sound of the slamming gate ring in my ears again like it had since the first day I heard it.

"Would you like to go back and sing with the others?"

Trying not to cry, trying not to react at all, I opened my mouth to answer, but nothing came out.

Not my "No."

Not any sound at all.

"Here's another chair," Miss Ritz pointed to the other side of her desk. "Why don't you sit with us for a bit?"

Miss Ritz opened the file folder on her desk. She paged through the papers and then turned them over again to read each page, slowly, while my mother sobbed quietly into her lap. Her chair sat at an awkward angle near the wall instead of next to mine where it belonged.

Concentrating on the chairs worked only for a moment. Everything that happened before I came to the home bombarded my thoughts.

I remembered waking up to find a cake on the table with "Happy Birthday, Debbie, 12 years old," written in blue letters across the smooth white frosting. I'd swiped a taste off the side and ran into Gram's room to thank her. But Gram wasn't there. Before I could figure out why, Uncle Lloyd came bursting in.

"What are you doing in here?" he'd asked. "My mother is gone. Her heart gave out, and it's all Carol's fault." He grabbed my arm and added, "And yours." Then he shoved me out of the room and slammed the door.

I stood looking at that door. Gram had painted it yellow, her favorite color. I could see the brush strokes, and I could hear strange
strangled sounds coming from inside.

Ever since Uncle Lloyd came home from the war and he'd had to
sleep on the orange velveteen davenport, he'd been mad. Mad at Gram
for letting us move in when Daddy went back to Korea. Mad like he
wanted Gram all to himself to take care of him and his wounded hip
without my mother and me there, too.

Gram hadn't complained about cooking and cleaning for all of
us, but anyone could see it was too hard for her. So, without being
asked, I dried the dishes, put the clothes through the wringer when
the washing machine stopped, and swept the steps.

My mother never even tried because, ever since Daddy left for
Korea, all my mother did was lay on Uncle Lloyd's davenport all day
with the brown and yellow afghan spread over her. Until the day after
my ninth birthday when she got the telegram.

She had started to read it out loud. "We regret to inform you . . . "
but, she stopped, and no one ever told me what else it said. No one
told me why my mother ran out of the house without a coat or even
shoes. No one told me where she'd been before Uncle Lloyd found
her. I heard him tell Gram he'd taken her to the hospital, but I didn't
know why until Gram had tucked me into bed with tears in her eyes.

"I'm sorry, my sweet girl," Gram said. "Your daddy is gone up to heaven."

"But I want him here," I said.

Gram brushed the hair off my forehead and held her hand against
my cheek. "He was such a good daddy and loved you so much. The
best thing you can do now is to remember all the wonderful times
you had together."

But I couldn't do that, not right then.

Two days later, my mother got home. She went back to lying on the davenport but with the radio blaring and a drink in her hand. She made them with Pepsi like she thought no one would know what she added because we couldn't see it. Like she thought no one would notice how she couldn't talk without slurring every word.

And, it seemed like no one did because no one, not even Gram, ever said anything about it. All Gram said was, "My poor Carol. It's too much." Which didn't make sense to me because Gram was always the one who said, "God never gives us more than we can handle." And, Gram handled her part taking care of all of us. Until my twelfth birthday.

The day after my birthday, Uncle Lloyd had shaken my shoulder to wake me up. "Shhh," he shushed. "Don't wake your mother. She needs her sleep." Then he swept all my things off the dresser between our twin beds into a cardboard box and set it in the middle of the floor. "Put the rest of your things in here and get dressed," he said. "I'll be back to get you in a few minutes to take you there."

"Where?" I had wanted to shout. "Where are you taking me?" But, I didn't. I folded clothes into the box and held my Elizabeth Anne like I was still seven-years-old until he came back. He picked up the box without a word, and I followed him. In the back seat of the car, I tried to pay attention to where we were going, but there were too many turns and too many streets I'd never seen before. After Uncle Lloyd left me at The Home, I hadn't seen him or my mother again, not even once. Until tonight.

My thoughts rolled like a scary movie in my head. I don't know how long I sat there staring at nothing, never turning my eyes to my mother. It seemed like I sat there forever and only a moment at the same time.

A knock sounded on the door, and I shifted my eyes. Uncle Lloyd. Keeping my face turned away, I could still see his brown wingtips, shinier than ever, move into the office so I let my eyes move up. The knife-edge crease in his trousers looked crisper than it used to. Under his gray fedora, which he didn't bother to take off, his face looked sad, maybe even kind. He didn't say a word as he scooped Mother up like a baby, but, going out to the door, he left a soft, "Thank you" behind. That "thank you" seemed so unlike the Uncle Lloyd I remembered from the last time I saw him.

I sat in the chair without moving while Miss Ritz closed the file folder and put it in the gray metal file cabinet behind her desk. Turning to me, Miss Ritz spoke with a gentle voice, "I believe the children have gone up to get ready for the Christmas Eve service at church. Are you ready to join them?"

What happened to supper? I wasn't hungry, but I hadn't heard anyone pounding up or down the stairs. Where had the time gone? I didn't know, and I didn't care because my insides were dead. Murdered by my mother.

Going to church where it was quiet, I could think things through but not with all the people celebrating Christmas Eve singing and happy. I couldn't stand there singing, not with my dead heart. I couldn't be with anyone, so I looked up at Miss Ritz with pleading eyes.

"Come with me, dear." Miss Ritz led me through the empty foyer where everything had gone wrong, around the tree, and past the television with its blank screen. I tried to think of Lassie's happy family, but my thoughts had died, too.

Once we were in the back hall, I saw the open door to the infirmary ahead, and my mind went completely blank.

CHAPTER TWENTY-ONE

UNLIKELY

"Debbie, wake up." Putting away my dreams, I recognized Patricia's voice.

I blinked at the bright bulb of light dangling from a ceiling much higher than the Big Girls' Room. For a moment, I forgot where I was and why, but then it all filled my thoughts like a wild, thundering storm. After all that awfulness, Miss Ritz had brought me here to the infirmary and helped me get into the bed. My mother's slurred voice came back in a rush as if it had traveled from deep inside, "Shh-ee my daww-ter."

Covering my face, I rolled away from Patricia. Unspeakable memories barged into my brain: the beautiful Christmas tree, the joyful singing, and the front door crashing open. I couldn't bear to think of all that happened.

How could I ever face anyone again?

The bed squeaked when Patricia perched on the edge of it and patted my arm. Moments passed. Moments filled with thoughts I didn't want to think.

"I know you don't believe it," Patricia said. "But everything will be okay."

A tear rolled across the bridge of my nose followed by a silent stream, and my breath filled my chest in jerky gasps. I pulled up the crisp white sheet, pressing it against my face, and forced a word out. "How?"

"First of all, no one will say anything," Patricia said. "They're too excited about Christmas. When they got back from church a few hours ago, they all found three packages on their bed."

Three gifts? I wanted to say the words, but they stayed in my head.

"Eileen and I have been wrapping gifts for hours this last week. New underwear, of course, and the mittens knitted by the ladies' group at church. I picked out matching ones for you and Mary Ellen. Red. I'll let the third gift be a surprise."

As Patricia talked, I felt my breathing slow down almost to normal.

"I will tell you the surprise gifts came from the church ladies, too. They had a bake sale a few weeks ago, and the money went toward gifts for all of you. Miss Ritz did the shopping." Patricia spoke like she knew how much her talking as if nothing terrible had happened was calming me. "Sometimes it seems like that woman can accomplish more than is humanly possible. Yes siree, everyone was excited that's for sure. Except for Beverly. She's acting like a brat because the gifts she got weren't good enough for her. She must have been so spoiled before she came here. But I guess that makes it extra hard for her now."

I turned over. I'd never thought of that, maybe being spoiled did make it harder.

Patricia smoothed back my hair. "I need to get you upstairs. After Miss Ritz brought you here, she came and found me. She asked me to stay late and even gave me cab fare. She said I should let you sleep till eleven o'clock." Patricia glanced at her Timex. "Wow, it's already twenty minutes after. You sit tight. I'll be back in a jiff."

A moment later Patricia handed me a cool wet washcloth. "Press this against your eyes, and then I'll make sure you get up to bed all right."

The washcloth felt good. "Thank you," I said. As those words left my lips, they echoed through my mind in Uncle Lloyd's voice bringing back the thoughts I wanted to keep away. Uncle Lloyd's "thank you" to

Miss Ritz seemed different. Way different from the way he was when he came home from the war. Then, he was angry all the time. Maybe now he was more like he'd been before the war. Maybe.

As if she heard my thoughts, Patricia put her hand on my arm and squeezed. "I don't know if Miss Ritz would want me to tell you this, but, when I was in her office while she was getting the cab fare for me, the phone rang. I'm sure it was your uncle. Miss Ritz told him she thought AA was a wonderful idea," Patricia said. "AA stands for *Alcoholics Anonymous* where they help people like your mother. It won't happen overnight, but, if she sticks with it, you'll see, everything will be okay. I really do think it will be."

Standing up, I forced a smile because Patricia deserved it. Then, pressing her finger over her lips, she led the way upstairs past all the sleeping girls in the dormitory to the Big Girls' Room where Noreen breathed quietly, and Sharon snored. Patricia patted my arm and left without a sound.

A full moon shone through the window like a beam of blessings covering Sharon and creating a bright path across the room to my bed. Three packages sat waiting in the middle of my blue bedspread. Each one was wrapped in colored tissue, one red, one white, and one green. They were all tied up in yellow ribbon with lots of curls looking like a Christmas celebration all on their own. I hung my dress on my hook and slipped on my blue pajamas. Climbing under the covers, I was careful not to knock the packages off my bed. And, even more careful to keep any ugly thoughts out of my head.

The white package had seven new pairs of white cotton underwear with D. Spencer neatly printed under the label. Ripping open the green package, I smiled at the red cable-stitched mittens. Mary Ellen would be so pleased to see we had the same color.

I could tell by the shape and size what was in the red package. A book. I opened it slowly and read the title below the gold Newbery sticker on the cover, *Miracles on Maple Hill*. In a snowy scene below the title, a girl leaned against a big tree. Even without leaves, I knew it had to be like my favorite tree at school, a Maple because of the little bucket dangling off the trunk. The girl was close to my age but wore a very nice red coat, the kind a girl's parents would make sure she had instead of an ugly brown one.

Snuggling under the covers, I held up the book to catch as much of the moonlight as I could and began to read.

Mother, say the scoot-thing again,' Marly said.

Marly, such a nice name, and she had a mother. The mother sounded crabby, but she called her "dear" in the next paragraph and was sitting right next to Daddy.

One silent tear spilled down my cheek as I closed the book. Nothing was fair. If only my mother was just crabby, and my Daddy had come home from the war. I made up my mind that I would not think about any of that anymore. Nothing had changed.

This new book could keep my thoughts off all that. The girl on the cover with the red coat had a smile on her face but was alone leaning against that big Maple tree. Maybe she wanted a little sister, too. Opening the book, I began reading again at the beginning.

I woke with a start. My mouth was dry, and my new book had tumbled onto the floor. Scooping it up, I thought of Marly. I liked her, but we were not alike. Refusing to think about her family, I reminded myself that she didn't have any friends. I had Noreen and Sharon and Doris and my almost little sister, Mary Ellen. Mostly, I decided that we were different because I had the outing, which would surely make my life perfect.

CHAPTER TWENTY-TWO

UNCANNY

Christmas Day passed quietly with most of the girls spending time reading their new books. Everyone ignored Beverly's complaints. Her Highness expected to get better gifts than cheap underwear, ugly mittens, and a copy of *Ginger Pye,* a book she'd already owned. We could all ignore her, but, unfortunately, we couldn't stop hearing her. The rest of us appreciated the gifts we got, still none of us had much to say concerning Christmas.

Every time we had the door to the Big Girls' Room closed, Sharon whispered about the upcoming outing. Would it be only couples, or would they bring their families? She hoped she'd get taken out by a family with a couple of cute boys her age. I didn't comment because I knew that wasn't very likely. I did ponder the idea of a family who had lost a girl my age being there thinking maybe they'd want another girl to fill the hole in their family. I could hope.

Sunday finally rolled around. The weather had gotten warmer every day since Christmas making everyone dawdle along the way. Boys stomped in the puddles making the girls in line next to them squeal. I followed Mary Ellen who splashed enough to keep me a few extra feet behind her.

As soon as we walked into church, I noticed the hymn board. The first song was number 267, and I smiled because I knew the Christmas hymns started at number 250, and I loved to sing Christmas songs. I recognized number 267, but it took a moment to remember what song it was. And then I couldn't breathe. Number 267 was "Silent Night."

I stumbled on nothing trying to act normal. Paul caught my elbow and kept me steady all the way to the front pew on the left. Standing in the side aisle, Eileen was yelling in a whisper at Patricia because of all the puddle splashing so neither of them noticed me.

Please God, I prayed, *help me to . . . do this . . . and to not . . . fall apart.*

Patricia nudged me over and began paging through a hymnal. My throat got so tight I couldn't swallow. Closing the hymnal, she slid it back into the rack in front of us next to a Bible. Then she took my hand and pulled me down the aisle to the back of church, through the vestibule, and into the ladies' room.

"Thank you for coming with me," she said through a stall door. "Eileen is probably livid that we left right when the service started, but, don't worry, I'll make sure she knows I dragged you along as a cover for using the Ladies."

Patricia stayed in the stall longer than I expected she ought to while all I heard was muted organ music until she flushed. Then, as if she had all the time in the world, she washed her hands, dried them thoroughly, leaned toward the mirror, slowly wiped the corners of her eyes, smoothed her hair, and fluffed it up a bit. Each movement so quiet and careful, I began to feel calm.

The organ music stopped, and she snatched up my hand. "Let's hurry in while Pastor's praying so we don't distract anyone," she said pulling me along again.

Opening the sanctuary door quietly, Patricia gave me a wink. Sure enough, everyone's eyes were closed as the prayer floated through the hushed room. Except Eileen, of course. She craned her neck and glared back at us, but Patricia stepped between Eileen's glare and me until we slipped past her and into our seats. I focused on listening to the message covering details new to me about the kings searching for baby Jesus. By the time the organ started up for the last hymn, "O, Little Town of Bethlehem," I was able to sing along quietly.

Paul eyed me as we marched out of church, and I mouthed, "Thank you."

Trudging up the girls' stairs when we got back to The Home, I noticed in the parlor that the tree was gone, and I was glad. Still, thinking of the tree made me remember Christmas Eve and my mother. I pulled in a calming breath; the smell of pine was even gone. Without the tree, maybe everyone else would forget what happened. Maybe.

Moments after the last boy marched in and started up the boys' stairs, the door banged open bashing the wall harder than it ever did for me.

A tall elegant couple stood in the doorway looking around the foyer. Both wore their long fur coats open showing off their expensive looking clothes. The woman had straight blonde hair much longer than any woman I'd ever seen. Her gaze swept over all of us on the stairs.

"There she is." The woman pointed halfway up the girls' staircase right at Beverly. Her haughty eyes dismissed the rest of us as if we were trash. In a crisp, accented voice, she said, "Beverly, my dear, I was afraid we'd never find you." Glancing over her shoulder at the man, she said to him, "I told you she would be here."

Looking down her nose at all of us, she clutched the huge collar of her fur coat over a cluster of pearl necklaces like she needed to hide them from us. She held a long gold cigarette holder between her fingers with bright red fingernails so long they made me wonder how she could even dress herself. I wouldn't have been surprised if she didn't.

Miss Ritz appeared at the bottom of our stairs. "Excuse me," she said standing her tallest. Before the woman could protest, Miss Ritz grasped her elbow and maneuvered her toward the office.

"Beverly, don't just stand there. Come along," the man said. He had the same accent as the woman, which made both of them sound superior to all of us.

The man hurried along behind Miss Ritz. "This child is my wife's niece. We've been out of the country for quite some time and only arrived in Chicago yesterday."

Beverly looked down her nose at all of us, buttoned her red coat up to the lambswool collar, and followed them.

We could hear Miss Ritz tell the three of them, "Take a seat. You will wait here until I am available." She closed the office door with more force than necessary.

We were all stock-still on the stairs. Miss Ritz stood with the front door behind her leisurely clasping her hands at her waist as if she intended to take as long as she pleased to give her simple instructions to us. In a pleasant voice she said, "Everything here is under control. Go ahead and continue on to your rooms."

After we'd put away our coats, Mrs. Petersen rang her bell. "You may all go to the game room or wait here until eleven o'clock when the boys come in from the play yard and it's our turn outside."

In the game room, instead of clamming up when I got near, all the girls wanted to talk about Her Highness and her hoity-toity relatives.

"Looks like Little Miss 'I'm so special' will be leaving," Sharon said.

It was no surprise to me. Beverly's exit would be as abrupt and unexpected as her arrival barely three weeks ago.

"Just so she's gone," one of the girls said. "That's all I care about."

Her comment was followed by lots of "me toos" and nods of agreement.

Almost everyone laughed out loud when Sharon said, "And, no one gives a diddley-squat how it happened."

But the truth was I wanted to know. In fact, I felt I should get to know after all the trouble I'd had with her living at The Home. It hadn't taken long to figure out kids were never told anything here. Nobody cared what we thought and that was not likely to change.

"I just hope she's really gone for good," Diane said.

Nancy gave a little snort. "I say, good riddance."

Linking arms with Nancy, Diane added, "Good riddance to bad rubbish."

Everyone laughed.

Maybe things were looking up. It seemed almost as if everyone had forgotten Christmas Eve. And, best of all, it looked like Beverly was long gone.

On Wednesday night, which was December 31, a glum mood spread through the dining hall. No surprise, we did not celebrate the New Year, but we knew everywhere else people were happy and excited to ring out the old year and ring in the new. The year 1958 had ended so terribly awful for me that 1959 had to be better. And, with the secret outing getting closer every day, something wonderful could happen. Even for me.

When we were dismissed from supper, Paul called over to Noreen, "See you next year." Lucky for him, none of the adults heard, and the sound of Noreen laughing was a great way to end the old year and anticipate the new one, trusting Jesus.

CHAPTER TWENTY-THREE

UNTOLD

On Monday, as soon as school was in sight, I spotted Doris by our Maple.

"Hi Doris," Mary Ellen said before skipping off to the side door.

It wasn't necessary to walk Mary Ellen to school anymore since Beverly was gone, but I liked spending that time with my almost little sister.

"Look, what I got for Christmas." Doris held out a green pen.

"It looks like a really nice fountain pen," I said.

I'd thought that I would tell Doris all that happened since I'd last seen her, but now I couldn't. Not without crying at school.

"But, it's not," Doris said. "That's why I love it. I've never liked the way it feels to write with a ball point pen.

Confused because I hadn't been paying attention, I took the pen and examined it.

"It's called a cartridge pen," Doris showed me the little vial of ink that fit inside. It writes exactly like a fountain pen, but you don't fill it from an ink bottle. I always make a mess when I'm doing that."

"Nice," I said.

"How was your Christmas?" As soon as the words were out of her mouth, Doris looked away like she was sorry for asking. She probably realized Christmas at The Home wouldn't be much fun.

"We all got a couple of gifts."

"That's nice." Doris smiled at me, but I could see the pity in her eyes.

The bell rang. We both hurried to get in line and faced front. Up ahead, I saw a fancy red coat with a black lambswool collar.

"Is that Beverly?" I whispered.

"Looks like her," Doris whispered back. "With all her little fifth-grade fans."

"But, that's impossible."

"What do you mean?" Puzzled, Doris looked over her shoulder at me.

"The Sunday after Christmas, Beverly's highfaluting aunt and uncle showed up right after church and snatched her away like The Home was a disgusting dungeon or something worse."

"Maybe they live in this school district," Doris whispered.

The line started to move. I nodded, to be sure she'd know I heard her, but my eyes were on Beverly disappearing into Hirsch Elementary School. My school. What in the world was going on?

At the classroom door, Mr. Kelly stood flashing his dimples at everyone. "Welcome back," he said to each student. He smiled right at Doris as if he meant it for both of us, but I knew it wasn't for me.

As soon as everyone in class was at their desk, Mr. Kelly stood in the front of the blackboard waiting for silence. "I trust everyone had a terrific Christmas vacation." He flashed his dimples around the room. "Starting today, we have a new music teacher."

Spinning around to the blackboard, Mr. Kelly picked up the chalk. Right below January 5, 1959, he wrote, Thursday, March 26, 1959. Without turning he said, "Please take out your composition books and write this on your next clean page." Then he slowly wrote E. He held the chalk in midair for a moment. He added A.

I focused on my composition book. It was the only way I could keep from letting out a loud sigh what with Mr. Kelly writing all dramatic like that. My next clean page was way more than halfway through the book after scads of pages covered with "I will not this" and "I will not that." It seemed like Mr. Kelly wanted me to behave like a robot with no feelings at all. What would he say if he knew writing all those sentences didn't change my thinking one iota?

Doris and I made eye contact. Crossing my fingers, I held them up with a hopeful expression. Doris crossed hers with a grin. I knew we both hoped the new music teacher would be better than Mrs. O'Hare. She'd always been crabby.

I wrote Thursday, March 26, 1959, at the top of a fresh page. Mr. Kelly had moved over, keeping us from seeing the rest of what he was writing. He held his chalk midair for a moment. The whole class had been holding their breath; so, when he turned around revealing "Easter Concert," everyone took in a loud breath.

Facing the class, Mr. Kelly said, "Parents and relatives are invited to attend." His eyes started their usual slide over to me whenever anything related to families came up in class. I looked down and wrote EASTER CONCERT in capital letters.

"Our class will practice during regular music period on Thursday mornings," Mr. Kelly said. "In order to have sufficient time for practice, we will forgo our Monday afternoon films until after Easter vacation. During that time, all our seventh and eighth classes will practice together in the auditorium. Both grades will sing three songs together."

The classroom erupted in excited voices.

"Three songs, that's a lot!"

"Do we all have to sing?"

"Will there be solos?"

"Boys and girls, please," Mr. Kelly said. "I am certain all your questions will be answered during today's practice. Now, take out your Social Studies books and turn to page 182."

Solos? I hadn't thought of that. Mrs. O'Hare hadn't assigned any solos for the Christmas concert. Just small special parts like Roberta got. If there were solos, even I might get to do one. It was hard to concentrate on Social Studies with so much bouncing around in my head.

At exactly ten minutes to two, Mr. Kelly stood up from his desk and said, "Please clear your desks. Gather what you need to take home, leave those items on top of your desk, and line up."

Sitting down, he acted like he didn't notice all the whispering and hurried banging of books. Once in a while, Mr. Kelly did let us act like kids. My heart had started to beat faster as soon as he gave the directions. Was I being foolish to hope for a solo?

Maybe, the new music teacher would assign solos. Unless, maybe parents had to attend for a girl to get a solo. Lots of things at school were unfair like that, but I could have new parents by then since the outing was coming up over a month before Easter. Or maybe there was some other reason I couldn't imagine. Still, stepping into the hall, it seemed impossible not to hope.

CHAPTER TWENTY-FOUR

UNSURE

My first impression of the auditorium hit me smack dab in the nose the moment Mr. Kelly marched our class through the massive double doors. The smell of dust and some kind of grease hung in the air. Our parade traveled down the aisle between row after row of maroon velvety seats and right up the steps onto the stage. Mr. Kelly stopped before my end of the line got to the steps. He moved aside and directed us to line up across the stage in one long row. I ended up near the middle, and, somehow, Doris was next to me.

Music filled the air coming from the upright piano sitting at an angle near the front of the stage with the back facing us and showing its wooden insides. The song was lively, but I didn't recognize it.

"Look," Doris whispered nodding toward the piano player who stood up and smiled over the piano at our class. "That's my fifth-grade teacher. She likes everyone, even kids from The Home unlike . . . " Her eyes followed Mr. Kelly as he left the stage and took a seat third-row center.

The other seventh-grade class arrived filing across the stage in front of our class. Then, the two eighth-grades made two more rows in front of ours. How would Miss Bailey ever hear me sing from way in the back of all these kids?

Doris elbowed me looking worried, too. "Sing loud," she whispered.

"Good afternoon, ladies and gentlemen, my name is Miss Bailey." She stopped playing and stood behind the piano. "Some of you may recognize me from when you were in my class for fifth-grade. I'm delighted to see each one of you. Let's get started immediately. Please face forward as you are. I'll arrange everyone after I hear you sing."

Miss Bailey began playing another song that I recognized right away, "How Great Thou Art," one of my favorites. Half standing to peer over the top of the piano, she said, "Everyone who knows this song please sing out so the others can hear the words clearly and learn them." She sat and played the introduction reaching one hand up and pointing at us when it was time to start singing.

On the first words, "Oh, Lord, my God, when I in awesome wonder," I was one of the few who sang. Soon enough, others joined in, and, by the third time through, almost everyone sang the chorus without a problem. At first, only a few of us knew the second and third verses, but, by the second time through, lots of kids caught on and sang most of the words.

"That was wonderful," Miss Bailey said. She got up and came around the piano. "I am so looking forward to our upcoming performance. Now that I've heard how well you did with this song, I am expecting it will be a fabulous concert."

Miss Bailey walked slowly back and forth in front of us making eye contact with me and other kids as she spoke. "The song you just sang began as a beautiful poem written by Carl Gustav Boberg in Sweden almost 75 years ago. It will be the perfect finale for our concert."

Several kids raised their hands, but Miss Bailey glanced at each of them and continued. "The first song you will sing is 'Easter Parade' because it fits the occasion, and I do believe we can impress our audience by singing it in harmony. Our second selection, 'It Might as Well be Spring' is . . . " She paused and smiled. "Well, just for fun. And I'm hoping to have at least a half dozen of you singing a line solo."

My breath caught in my throat.

Miss Bailey headed back to the piano. "But first we have to start at the beginning. I need to hear each one of you sing, so I know how to divide you into three sections. Soprano, alto, and hopefully enough of you boys to fill a section at tenor." Still standing, she played the first measures of "How Great Thou Art." She pointed at the girl who stood closest to the piano in the first row. "Starting with you, I want each one to come up, tell me the number of your classroom, your name, and then sing the chorus for me."

A hushed buzz of excitement, or was it nerves, rose from all of us.

"That'll separate the men from the boys," Doris whispered. "But at least we don't have to worry about her hearing us."

The first girl went up with sluggish jerky steps like her feet were taking her somewhere she didn't want to go.

"Students, please give each other the courtesy of your silence."

In an instant, you could almost hear a pin drop, but it was still impossible for me to hear the first girl when she whispered her room number and name. Then, even though she sang too quietly, I could tell she wasn't quite on-key.

When the girl finished, Doris elbowed me and made googly eyes, which did not make me feel like giggling. What if I couldn't sing like I usually did? I kept my eyes front. Biting my bottom lip, I prayed Miss Bailey would understand how important this was to me. Maybe if I got a solo and sang it well, the new family I was sure to get from the outing would learn to love me.

Miss Bailey finished writing on some paper on top of the piano. "Thank you, Phyliss. Next please."

And so, it went on, one after another, the girls and boys sang for Miss Bailey. Sometimes she cocked her head and listened to all four lines of the chorus. Other times she nodded and used her "Thank you" to stop them after the first two. Once or twice her "Thank You" interrupted the first line.

Straining to hear, I tried to tell if they were on-key or not. I couldn't always hear well enough to figure out why Miss Bailey stopped them when she did. When the first row was finished, Miss Bailey told them they could leave. Their teacher led them up the aisle and out the double doors.

Doris gave me a hopeful smile. I gave her a grateful one. It was good to have a friend who understood that a girl just had to succeed even when it seemed so unlikely.

By the time the second row was half done, each "Thank you" made my throat get drier and drier while my heart beat faster and faster. How would I be able to sing at all when my turn finally came? Gram had always said she loved the sound of my singing, but what would Miss Bailey think? I kept praying that God would help me do my very best.

When the other two classes were done, Jacob was the first one in our row. He stepped over to the piano. "Then sings my soul," he sang, but his voice cracked. He cleared his throat. On the second line his voice got stronger and better with each word, but Miss Bailey stopped him before he got to the fourth line.

I'd heard how he sang the right note and held it perfectly on his second "How great Thou art" which lots of kids had messed up. As far as I was concerned, Jacob sang better than anyone else who'd been loud enough for me to hear so far. But then, why did Miss Bailey stop him?

One after another, kids I saw every day in school went up and sang. Roberta was absolutely awful, but her smile when she walked back looked like she thought she was the best singer in the whole class. Then Doris went up. I was next. What if my dry throat made me sound worse than Roberta? Desperate, I gathered up as much spit as I could and sloshed it back and forth in my mouth. Then, Miss Bailey was saying "Thank you, Doris."

Somehow, I made it up to the piano. "Room 209," I said with a shaky voice. "Debbie Spencer." That was better. I closed my eyes, waiting for the sound of the piano. How would I ever sing well enough to earn a solo?

Gram's voice pierced my thoughts. "With God, nothing is impossible."

Smiling, I listened for the sound of the first measure. I forgot about Doris and Roberta and Miss Bailey. Instead, I thought of the words and sang each one as a prayer.

Opening my eyes, I watched Miss Bailey's hand moving over the paper on top of the piano. She'd let me sing the whole chorus without stopping me, and, now, she was already finished writing.

With the same smile she gave everyone, Miss Bailey said, "Thank you, Debbie. Next, please."

Walking back to the line, my heart stopped beating all together, and I forgot all about my song being a prayer. I tried to swallow, but I had nothing to swallow. I couldn't look at Doris.

I was sure Miss Bailey had written "off-key."

CHAPTER TWENTY-FIVE

UNEXPECTED

Leaving school, Doris and I couldn't overlook the long, black limousine sitting out front. A guy with a funny little hat closed the back door, got into the driver's seat, and drove off.

"That was Beverly," Doris said. "I saw her red coat. The one she thinks makes her look so jimp."

"Ha, that's true," I said. "I just don't get why she's still here at Hirsch."

"From what you told me about how her aunt and uncle acted, I expected her to go to some la-di-da private school," Doris said. "Why would anyone with a ride like that go here?"

"Good question."

Mary Ellen skipped up to us. "What question?"

"Never mind." I looked at Doris, and she wiggled her eyebrows back at me.

Adding a hop to her skip, Mary Ellen set off toward Spaulding.

The limousine took a right at the corner of Homan. At least, it wasn't heading to The Home.

"You know," Doris said. "I read in the paper all the kids from Our Lady of the Angels are going to other schools while they rebuild. Maybe, Beverly still lives somewhere in this district and—"

"There wasn't any room in the private schools," I said finishing Doris' thought. "That could be it."

"It does make sense."

"As long as she leaves Mary Ellen alone," I said. "I don't care where Her Highness goes to school."

Doris laughed.

We followed Mary Ellen. She hop-skipped from the sidewalk to the snow along the edge. I dreaded hearing Doris' opinion of the concert practice, and, at the same time, longed to hear what she thought of my singing. I knew for certain Doris would be frank, but could I stand it without falling apart?

"Can you believe how awful Roberta sings?" Doris asked before we got to the corner. "Jacob was amazing. I used to think his hair was too long and curly for a boy, but, when he was singing, he looked so cute." Doris put her hand on my arm. "I'm dying to hear how you think I did."

Heat rushed to my face and ears. I hadn't listened to Doris' singing. Did I dare tell her the truth? "Oh, Doris, I know I should have listened carefully and tried to judge what Miss Bailey wrote down for you, but, the truth is—" I hesitated. Could I be completely honest? I didn't want to hurt Doris' feelings.

Doris squeezed my arm like she was trying to wring an opinion right out of me.

"I'm really sorry," I blurted out. "I don't remember yours what with me being next. I'm such an awful friend."

"You? What about me?" Doris asked. "After I sang, I was so worried about what Miss Bailey had written down I didn't pay any attention to you either."

Staring right into Doris' eyes, I held my breath. I couldn't tell how she felt until she burst out laughing. Relieved, I joined her laughing so hard I couldn't talk.

Doris couldn't seem to talk either covering her mouth and laughing into her hands.

Mary Ellen stopped and looked at us like we were crazy. "What's so funny?" she asked. When neither of us could answer, she shrugged and went back to hop-skipping.

"Aren't we a pair?" I finally got out. "But you must have been good or, at least, not bad. I would've noticed if you were bad."

"Do you think I was better than Roberta?" Doris bit her lip holding back a fresh giggle.

"Everyone was better than Roberta," I said. "Did you see the look on her face when she came back to the line?"

"Uh-huh," Doris said. "If only she had heard herself."

The two of us started in laughing all over again.

Catching my breath, I said, "Now we have to wait until music class on Thursday to find out how we did."

"I don't know how we'll do it."

"Me neither." I copied Mary Ellen's hop-skipping. "But, thanks anyway. Thinking you were listening and rooting for me made it easier."

"You're right." Doris hop-skipped. "I probably did better because you were there, too."

Mary Ellen stopped at the corner of Spaulding and Evergreen where we went our separate ways. "Why were you laughing so much?" she asked.

I took her hand and led her across the street calling goodbye to Doris.

Doris called back, "See you tomorrow."

"What was so funny?" Mary Ellen asked.

"It's hard to explain," I said. "I guess it's not really funny. It's just fun to have a good friend."

"Oh-h." Clearly Mary Ellen didn't have a clue what I meant, but she pulled me along with a hop-skip anyway.

Before Noreen and Sharon even got their coats off, I closed the door and blurted out, "Beverly is still going to Hirsch."

"What?" Sharon said.

"Hmm," Noreen said. "That's a surprise."

"It sure is," Sharon said. "Why wouldn't her la-di-da aunt and uncle send her to a private school?"

"I don't know," I said. "But she was there." I couldn't say that maybe the private schools were overfull now. Not with Noreen acting so normal.

"I'm going to ask Diane and Nancy. She was in their class, wasn't she?" Sharon opened the door. "I'll be right back with the facts."

A moment later, Sharon told us, "Diane said she'd acted like she always does, but Nancy did hear her bragging about her ritzy new place."

I had a feeling I wasn't finished dealing with Her Highness. Trying to figure out what was going on with her was a great distraction for my brain. For the rest of the afternoon, through dinner, and up until I was in bed, I didn't let myself think of the singing at all. But, in the dark, I couldn't hold back my thoughts.

Why didn't Miss Bailey stop me before I sang the whole chorus? She'd stopped Jacob who was a great singer. I was pretty sure Doris hadn't sung it all either since her turn was over so quickly. Maybe Miss Bailey didn't like my singing at all. I still hoped she liked Doris'. It seemed as if everything was going all wrong for me.

If only Christmas Eve had been different. If only my mother hadn't been drinking, she could have joined the circle and added her strong beautiful voice to our singing. She used to sing all the time, but that was before. Before Daddy went to Korea. Before he didn't come back. I squeezed my eyes tight to keep the tears in and buried my face in my pillow.

After a while I rolled over and looked out the window. Tiny snowflakes danced in the wind. I remembered Gram telling me that Daddy was in heaven and saying the best thing you can do now is to remember all the wonderful times you had together. But I couldn't even think of him without crying so I never did. Until now. I prayed for God to help me and let the snowflakes remind me of another night, a long time ago, when I saw the same kind of snowflakes outside the window of an El train.

I was only seven, but I remembered every moment. Daddy took "both his girls" to see the Marshall Field's tree on the Saturday after Thanksgiving. The train had jerked and swayed all the way downtown filled with the smell of damp wool and winter. Daddy whistled "Joy to the World" as we made our way down the steps from the El to the street. We must have looked like a perfect family holding hands with me in the middle, Mom's face lustrous like a mannequin with her red plaid slacks and the brown trapper jacket she'd had since high school and Daddy so tall and handsome with his dark hair and blue eyes.

We strolled down the sidewalk on State Street all the way to Field's while cars zoomed by splashing up dirty, melted snow. On the seventh floor in the Walnut Room, the smell of pine surrounded us and the fabulous tree so tall I was sure it was a hundred feet high. Daddy laughed and said it was actually forty-five feet tall.

On the way home, Mom and Daddy sat across from me holding hands and smiling at each other. I'd been so tired I closed my eyes and curled up on the train seat. They must have thought I fell asleep because Daddy carried me home all the way from the El to our apartment. His chin was scratchy against my forehead, and his hair smelled so good from the Brylcreem he used singing "a little dab will do ya" whenever he put it on.

Now I could almost feel his strong arms under my legs and across my back. And how he laid me on my bed, took my shoes off, and pulled the covers up to my chin. How he kissed the top of my head.

The last kiss Daddy ever gave me.

CHAPTER TWENTY-SIX

UNTRIED

The next morning, the audition song was running through my head when I woke up. Humming it, I got dressed.

"I like that song," Noreen said

"Then sings my soul," I sang out. "My Savior God, to Thee."

"What song is it?" Sharon asked.

"How great Thou art," I sang. "How great Thou art."

"Wow," Sharon said. "That was out of this world."

"Do you really think so?" I asked. "We're doing an Easter Concert this year." I did not mention that was because the Christmas concert had been canceled with Noreen listening. I hurried on. "We have a new music teacher, and she's planning to assign solos."

"You'll get one for sure," Noreen said.

We all heard Mrs. Petersen's bell for breakfast.

"I agree, don't ya know." Sharon opened the door to the dormitory.

I couldn't help but wonder if they were just being nice.

At school, everyone was talking about the upcoming Easter concert and who would sing the solos. In the line outside, Roberta told everyone she didn't want to sing a solo. Her mother said it's not right for a girl to show off like that.

Doris wiggled her eyebrows at me, which meant we knew the real reason Roberta's mother didn't want her to sing a solo in public.

Finally, Thursday morning did come, and, right after the pledge, Mr. Kelly marched us down to the music room, which was the same as any other classroom but without desks. Miss Bailey sat at the piano playing "Easter Parade." "Please gather together in a few rows at that end of the room," she said.

Finishing the song, Miss Bailey stood at the piano. "Today we are going to sing all three songs as many times as we can. Our goal is for everyone to memorize the words. Also, I won't be assigning solos today because I want to know who's interested and then decide how to arrange everything. I will announce the soloists first thing on Monday."

I swallowed my disappointment, and Doris frowned.

We sang "Easter Parade" twice, and, by then, most everyone was singing all the words. Then we did "How Great Thou Art" three times. It wasn't all that hard to learn either since a lot of us already knew it. "It Might as Well Be Spring" was a new song to all of us. We were singing it for the third time when I spotted Mr. Kelly leaning against the door frame.

Miss Bailey looked at her watch. "Oh my," she said. "It's time for you to go back to class. Let's all think of how we might change some of these words to make them more appropriate. We can talk about it on Monday."

With more commotion than Mr. Kelly ever allowed, the class got into a line.

"One more thing," Miss Bailey said. "On your way out, if you're interested in singing a solo, please stop at the blackboard and add your name to that list." She pointed to a list of names written under the word, *Solos*. "Both eighth-grades had music yesterday, but we still need more soloists."

I counted seven names on the list, before I added mine right below Jacob and Doris'.

Wishing I could remember all the words to the spring song, I tried to figure out how many solos there might be. There had to be at least ten. The other seventh-grade went past us in the hall on their way to music. I remembered several of them were good singers. The question was, how many of them would want a solo?

On the way home, Doris and I agreed it would seem like forever till Monday. But Monday did come, and Miss Bailey stood at the top of the stairs to the stage. "Boys and girls, as you come up please tell me your name. I will tell you if you are a soprano, an alto, or a tenor. Then please stand on the risers," she pointed to them. "Tenors in the center. Sopranos on the boys' right, as you face me. Altos on the left. You may stand where you'd like today, but I may rearrange some of you later."

I was pretty sure both Doris and I would be sopranos. Sure enough, when I gave my name to Miss Bailey, she said, "Soprano." I took a spot in the middle row with Doris standing next to me.

When the other classes arrived, Miss Bailey gave the same instructions. After everyone found a place, Miss Bailey said, "Now, if I call your name please move down to make a row in front of the risers. Doris Anderson, Mary Ann Bernardo, Nadine Burgman . . ."

What did being in the front row mean? Was it for kids singing a solo? It seemed like forever until I heard, "Debbie Spencer." Doris waved me to the spot next to her. Jacob Weinberg was the last name Miss Bailey called.

Then, true to form, Miss Bailey did not make anyone wonder why she had arranged us that way. "The front row is for our soloists. It looks like everyone who signed the list is there. Did I forget anyone?"

No one raised a hand, but some students gasped or let out quiet squeals or whispered to each other. Miss Bailey allowed us to react turning to her papers on top of the piano. After several minutes, she turned around. "William," she said to an eighth-grade boy. "Will you please roll that blackboard over here." She pointed off stage. When the blackboard was in place, we could all see the words to "It Might as Well be Spring" written in neat, easy-to-read script.

"Before I assign solos, we need to look at the words for this song." Then she squatted down and opened a brown box sitting on the floor next to the piano. It looked like a square suitcase but turned out to be a Victrola. "Let's listen, too." Swinging the arm over, she set the needle on the edge of the 78 spinning on the turntable.

The song started out slow. The woman on the recording sang of how she was mixed up, which made me think about how I felt lately. She sang lots of descriptions of her feelings, and I was sure those lines would be the solos.

When the song ended, Miss Bailey stopped the record. "This song was written by Rodgers and Hammerstein for the movie *State Fair* in 1945. You can see how each of these lines could be sung as a solo," Miss Bailey pointed. "It will make the whole song more lively and interesting. I've heard it sung starting with this line, 'I'm as restless as a willow in a windstorm,' but I like the beginning. Plus, I do believe we will change this line." She pointed to the one that said, "'From a (man or girl) I've yet to meet' is usually changed depending on whether a girl sings the song or a man."

Roberta's hand popped up.

"Yes, Roberta?"

"I don't think my mother will like me singing this song." Roberta used her haughty voice. "Not if it's about girls and boys dating."

"I realized that some parents might be concerned about that, and I've decided we will sing 'friend'." Miss Bailey acted like she didn't notice Roberta's tone of voice. She erased man or girl and wrote in "friend." "Will your mother be okay with that?"

Roberta nodded.

"I'd also like to include the first stanza," Miss Bailey continued, "but, we need to change those words a bit, too."

Doris raised her hand. At Miss Bailey's nod she said, "I think it should say 'Teacher' instead of 'Mama' since we are at school and all."

But I knew that wasn't Doris' only reason. Neither one of us wanted to sing about mothers. Certainly not in front of an audience that was bound to be filled with so many of them that weren't ours.

"Good idea." Miss Bailey erased "mama" and wrote "teacher." "What about the word 'dope'?"

Several kids shouted out their opinions.

"It isn't very nice."

"My mother wouldn't want me singing it."

"Mine neither."

Miss Bailey asked, "Does anyone have an idea of how we could change it?" She put her finger on her chin and let her eyes drift around the room.

At first, no one responded, which was silly as far as I was concerned. I could already tell Miss Bailey would never make anyone feel stupid for a suggestion. Out of the corner of my eye, I saw Roberta raise her hand at shoulder level, maybe because we weren't in our own classroom where she was always the favorite.

At the teacher's nod, Roberta quietly said, "'Hope' rhymes with 'mope'."

"Hmm . . . hope would be a good word, but the line has to fit the music and still make sense." She played the lines singing the words.

Roberta's hand went up all the way. "It could be 'pretending life is wonderful and knowing I can hope'."

"That's perfect!" Miss Bailey sang the lines through using Roberta's idea. "It looks like we have a real poet in our midst," she said.

Doris elbowed me and raised her eyebrows high enough to almost hide them under her bangs. I returned a look that said, *Roberta will really be a pain in the neck now.*

Referring to the papers on top of the piano, Miss Bailey began calling the names of the students in the first row and reading off their solo lines. I held my breath. I loved the line about being "vaguely discontented." If only I could sing that one, I'd do it perfectly. I was sure of it.

But Miss Bailey called out Sarah Ryan, a girl from an eighth-grade class to sing it. I stopped thinking of other lines I'd like to sing and tried to keep my face blank. Doris got the line with a giddy baby which I knew was perfect for her. I was starting to feel like my name would never be called. Why did Miss Bailey put me in the front row if she wasn't going to give me a solo? Maybe, my name hadn't been called to be on the front row. Maybe I'd imagined it because I so wanted a solo. But, then why had Doris waved me to the spot next to her instead of telling me I wasn't supposed to be there?

Listening to others getting a solo, my mouth went dry, and my throat got tight. And then, without reading a line, Miss Bailey called out Jacob's name, the only other student in the first row who hadn't been called. "Jacob, I'd like you to sing the next three lines," she said. "And the whole class will join you on the last one. We might work out some harmony for that line."

Closing my eyes, I felt my face growing red and hot. I couldn't breathe. I wasn't picked for a solo after all, and no one else seemed to notice, not even Doris. Maybe I should try to move back.

"Debbie," Miss Bailey said.

Was she sending me to the second row? No. She was looking right at me with a smile. Air rushed into my lungs—cool fresh air, that made my throat relax.

"I'd like you to be the one to introduce this song with your solo," she said. "Please try the first few lines." Going over to the piano, Miss Bailey sat and played a few measures and then sang the opening with, "pretending life is wonderful and knowing I can hope."

Something about singing those lines with the new class poet's words rubbed me the wrong way. But, after all my worry, it seemed silly so I let it go and listened carefully.

Closing my eyes, I didn't think of Roberta or my mother or anyone. I concentrated on my solo and sang with a clear voice right on key. Once I started, I didn't care a whit that Roberta thought up the new words. Instead, I felt each word. When I got to the last line, I fell in love with the words. "And knowing I can hope."

Because hope was for anyone. No matter where they lived.

CHAPTER TWENTY-SEVEN

UNEASY

For the next month, I kept busy practicing for the concert and daydreaming about the outing and my new family. I wasn't surprised when no one showed up to see me on Valentine's Day, and I didn't care because the only thing that made that day special was the day after it anyway.

On the way to church the Sunday after Valentine's Day, I made sure Paul was in the boy's line across the sidewalk from me.

"Could I ask you a favor?" I asked like I'd planned.

"Sure."

"Could you please think of something else when we pray The Lord's Prayer today? So you don't get yourself in trouble?"

"Just for the record it's supposed to be called 'The Our Father Prayer,'" Paul said. Then he laughed. "I guess telling the minister that wouldn't get past Miss Nielsen either. Anyway, what difference does it make if I do get in trouble?"

"Actually, I can't tell you." It would be impossible to tell Paul about the outing without someone else hearing. "But I'm positive you'll be glad you did."

"Quit your dawdling back there," Eileen yelled from the front of the line.

"Why does she always look back at us?" I said.

"I think she knew we'd be enjoying the nice weather," Paul said. "She just had to stop us."

I laughed.

After church, when we were filing back up the stairs to our dormitories, Miss Ritz came out of her office. She was hardly ever there on Sunday so everyone else must have been surprised to see her.

"Just a moment, girls and boys," she called out.

We stopped where we were.

"I have a special surprise for all of you." She glanced at her wrist watch. "You will not be having dinner here today."

Everyone began murmuring to each other. I caught Paul's eye in the boys' line. He winked.

As if we were silent, Miss Ritz went on, "At one o'clock, I would like all of you to gather in the front parlor. Please bring your coats and be ready for a special outing."

I thought my heart would pound out of my chest. This was it. The outing I'd been hoping and praying for was finally happening. My life would never be the same again.

When we got to the front parlor, I did not let the memory of the Christmas tree steal my joy. Instead, I smiled at the davenports sitting in their places along the walls with the coffee table in between. Chairs from the dining hall lined up against the walls giving everyone a place. Sitting in one of the chairs, I avoided eye contact with anyone by staring at the coffee table. I didn't dare let on that I already knew why we were all there.

The coffee table was much bigger and heavier than the one I remembered, but, still, my mother's voice came back to me from way before the slurring. Way before Daddy had even joined the Marines. Thinking of Gram telling me to remember Daddy, I let my thoughts go where they should.

"Don't mess them up," my mother had said with a laugh while I sat in Daddy's lap watching her straighten our coffee table. She carefully arranged four copies of *Life* magazine in a fan like a hand of cards when they played Rummy together.

"But what if I want to read one?" Daddy had asked swiping a magazine from the middle of the fan and making a mess of it.

"Stop, Bill." My mother laughed again, and Daddy had pulled her into a hug making a pile of us on his lap.

My heart pounded. If only I could have that family. But I knew it was gone forever, and I needed to forget all of it. Because, today, I was sure I'd find a new family that was perfect.

"Good afternoon, children," Miss Ritz's voice startled me interrupting my thoughts.

"In a few minutes, we will begin a very special outing. Special because it involves our whole community and is unlike any outing The Evergreen Home has ever hosted. Also, it is special because it is a memorial for the horrific event that will forever besmirch the history of this wonderful city." Miss Ritz paused to give a tender smile to Paul and then Noreen who was sitting next to me. Noreen had her hand in her pocket, no doubt rubbing her rosary.

Miss Ritz continued. "We have invited families in the community to select one of you and provide a pleasant outing for the afternoon and early evening. You will all return by seven o'clock. I expect each one of you to represent The Evergreen Home in a positive light."

"Miss Ritz," Sharon called out without raising her hand or anything.

"Yes, Sharon."

"Will these families want to adopt some of us?"

"Before anyone can adopt one of you," Miss Ritz said. "They have to go through the State of Illinois adoption process."

"So, that means they can't?"

"No," Miss Ritz answered patiently. "That means they could, but the process is complicated and lengthy."

Several girls and boys murmured. Sharon looked right at me clapping her hands silently in front of her excited smile. Why did Sharon always have to be so forward? And, why couldn't Sharon understand some people liked to keep some things private?

My heart beat like a huge parade drum. I looked down at my new favorite dress. The one with the shiny, dark turquoise bodice and even shinier striped skirt. I was excited that I'd gotten it before anyone else did yesterday.

I turned to Mary Ellen and said, "I hope a terrific family comes and wants to adopt you."

"But I'd miss you too much," Mary Ellen said.

"Children, please," Miss Ritz said in a quiet voice that encouraged everyone to settle down and focus on her.

"When the couples arrive, Mrs. Petersen and Miss Nielsen will greet them at the door and direct them to my office. I will meet with them for a short interview and some advice concerning whom they might choose. After seeing me, either Patricia or Eileen will escort them here and they will choose one of you. After they make their selection, Mrs. Bell will assist them in signing you out."

Miss Ritz gestured toward the doorway to the foyer where Mrs. Bell sat behind a folding table with a stack of papers in front of her. She straightened a row of pens that lay next to the papers.

"You may speak quietly to each other, but please remain in your seats." With that, Miss Ritz made her way to her office. The front parlor erupted with the clamor of children's voices.

Sharon leaned over Mary Ellen and started babbling, "This is going to be a blast. I hope I get to go to the Palmer House for dinner. Then a walk along the lake front would be nice."

"It's bound to get colder while we're out," Noreen said. "A museum would be nice."

"You're right. It is still winter," Sharon said. "But I don't want to go to a stuffy museum, don't ya know. Maybe I'll get to see a movie."

"You shouldn't look a gift horse in the mouth," Noreen said with a scowl.

"I never did understand what that means—"

Sharon's words got lost in Mary Ellen's outcry. "Look, Debbie!" She pulled on my skirt, pointing to several people coming in the front door. "Look!"

Like a wave, silence rolled around the room. Both boys and girls nudged their neighbors. We all stared at the visitors. Patricia spoke quietly to them as they stood waiting in the foyer sneaking glances into the front parlor.

Moments later, I held my breath as Patricia escorted the first couple into the room. They stood awkwardly smiling at each child until the husband's gaze stopped on one of the youngest boys. Tommy. As the three of them went to Mrs. Bell's check-out table, Eileen, looking as grumpy as ever, led the next couple into the room. I watched Tommy open the door for the first couple.

"There are so many of them." A quivery, old voice pulled my eyes back to the parlor.

Following Eileen, a short, gray-haired man said, "You choose, Myrtle."

"Oh, no, Howard. You are much better at making choices," the woman with him said. They were so close to the same size and shape, they could have been twins. She smiled at him making her wrinkles so joyful that I couldn't help but smile, too.

With their gray coats and black boots, they were hard to tell apart, except for the edge of a black dress peeking out from the bottom of one coat and black trousers from the other. Even their hats were almost the same. He held a small black bowler, and she wore a pill box without a net. Mary Ellen couldn't take her eyes off them. All I could see was how old they were. Way too old to adopt anyone.

Without so much as a nod in their direction, Eileen left the fusty couple standing in the middle of the front parlor. Looking a bit confused, the woman peered around the room. When she spotted Mary Ellen, she gasped, "Oh, Howard, look."

The old man stepped in front of Mary Ellen. He bowed from the waist and reached out a hand. She giggled and stood up to take it. He twirled her around. "My, my, you're the spitting image of her, you are."

"He means our daughter, Agnes," the old woman said. "She's all grown up, she is, and living in Seattle."

The couple seemed kind enough, but I was sure they were all wrong for Mary Ellen. If she couldn't be my sister, I at least wanted her to have the right kind of family. I looked over their heads at the next couple coming in. They looked perfect. The woman had dark hair fixed the same way my mother used to. The man was tall and strong looking. That couple moved ahead of Patricia and headed right toward me.

CHAPTER TWENTY-EIGHT

UNCLAIMED

"There you are, my dear," the woman said reaching out. She looked like the perfect mother.

I had almost lifted my hand when Noreen stood and took the woman's hand in both of hers.

"It's wonderful to see you, Mrs. Sullivan," Noreen said.

"And, where is Paul?" Mr. Sullivan spotted Paul who got up and shook hands with him.

"It's nice to see you," Paul said.

"We have special permission to take both of you, today," Mrs. Sullivan said giving Paul's arm a squeeze. "Carolyn and Lois are in the car. They couldn't wait till we got you home."

"I hope you don't mind," Mr. Sullivan said. "But the Mrs. has a big dinner in the oven. We thought we'd spend the time with you at home since the children want to see you, too."

"That would be wonderful." Noreen hadn't smiled like that in a long time.

"Will Patrick and Henry be home?" Paul asked as they headed over to Mrs. Bell.

"Oh, yes," Mrs. Sullivan said. "They're all hoping you'll play a game of Monopoly with them. They loved when you used to come over on a

Sunday and spend the whole day playing that game." Her voice faded away as they reached the doorway.

Swallowing my disappointment, I strained to hear their happy voices, my throat getting tight.

At the last moment, before they were out the door, Paul turned and gave me a wink. I gave him a little happy wave. He was so nice to me, and his wink gave me hope.

Watching Paul and Noreen with the Sullivans, I had missed the room filling up with all sorts of people. I'd missed a lot of chairs getting empty including the one next to mine. Mary Ellen's. I glimpsed the gray-haired man pushing open the front door for the gray-haired woman and Mary Ellen.

The smell of too many perfumes, wet galoshes, and wool coats made the whole room stuffy. Girls were sighing and giggling as they were picked, and boys whooped with joy. Mrs. Bell's table was surrounded by lots of adults and kids making it hard to tell who was coming in and who was going out.

Sharon barged over blocking my view. "There's scads of people in here. How can anyone see me?" she asked. "I'm moving over closer to the door."

It seemed like time moved faster than normal. I was sure Mary Ellen had been laughing as she left with the gray ones, but it seemed all wrong. They were too old to adopt anyone. Now, what would I do when my couple found me. I could never leave my little sister behind.

Sharon swept past me. "My coat is right over here," she said.

The couple who followed her looked really young. As they walked away, Sharon boldly told them she hadn't seen a movie in such a very long time.

"We'll have to remedy that," the young woman said with a big smile.

And then, the whole room was empty.

Alone at her table, Mrs. Bell lined her pens up in a neat row. No one except Mrs. Petersen and Miss Nielsen were in the foyer. Mrs. Petersen stepped outside and looked up and down the street. Back inside she quirked her eyebrows at Miss Nielsen. They both turned to the front parlor where I was the only one sitting in a chair.

The only one not chosen.

The only one still waiting for someone to want me.

Hot tears lurked behind my eyes. I pulled my eyebrows up and blinked hard. Taking a deep breath, I sat right where I was. Mrs. Bell gathered up the pens and the last of the papers. Eileen snatched up the table and tipped it over folding the legs with four sharp clacks. Patricia took the chair and folded it flat. They both followed Mrs. Bell toward the stairs to the dining hall. Miss Nielsen and Mrs. Petersen pulled on their coats and went out the front door.

What was I supposed to do? Wait in my chair until everyone returned? Go up to the Big Girls' Room?

Miss Ritz walked toward me buttoning her coat. "Debbie, my dear," she said. "You and I will have a special outing, too."

Stunned, I didn't know what to say. I couldn't get any words out anyway. My blinking and deep breathing had dried up my tears, but I knew they could surge back at any moment.

"Put on your coat and come along," Miss Ritz said. "A cab is on the way." She strode to the door acting like taking me out was the most natural thing in the world. Like I wasn't the only girl no one wanted.

Grabbing my coat, I pulled my thoughts into a tight knot and buttoned them shut like an ugly coat.

Miss Ritz peered out the window of the front door. "We will have dinner at The Palmer House," she said. "How would you like that?" She kept her back to me turning her head only a bit each way to look down the street.

Patricia and Eileen scurried around the parlor folding up the metal chairs and carrying them two at a time down the girls' stairs.

Glad that they weren't watching me, I fumbled with my coat. How did the sleeve get all twisted so a girl couldn't slip an arm in? I jerked the coat off my shoulders and stared at it.

Across the room Patricia stopped in the middle of folding a chair with a look of pity.

Grabbing the coat by the shoulders, I gave it a violent shake, shoved my arms in, and thrust the horrid brown buttons through their horrid holes all the way up to my neck. Just like I'd buttoned up my thoughts. My breath caught in my throat with a strangled shriek at the sight of the matching sister mittens that I pulled from my pocket.

Halfway through the girls' doorway, a chair under each arm, Eileen stopped at the sound. As she opened her mouth, Patricia plowed into her.

"Quit dawdling," Patricia said. She jerked her chin toward the stairs. "Let's finish up so we can get home."

"I got no reason to rush," Eileen said.

Patricia's voice was angry. "You could think about how others might feel just this once."

"And why should I ever do that?"

"Think of it as plain, old human decency."

"Humph."

"Come on," Patricia said. "These chairs aren't going to put themselves away."

Eileen's voice drifted back to the parlor from the stairs sounding almost wistful. "You got yourself a date, don't you?"

Patricia giggled.

CHAPTER TWENTY-NINE

UNSETTLED

Taking a loud breath in and out, I moved across the parlor to the foyer. "I'm ready."

"And here comes our cab." Holding the door open for me, Miss Ritz smiled. "Seems like it's getting colder."

I tried to smile back at her. Hurrying down the steps and through the gate, I let it clang behind me. Even the sound of the gate clanging shut didn't unbutton my thoughts. I slid into the cab.

The cabbie slammed the door and hopped into the front seat. "Oooh-eee," he said. "It's getting nippy out there." He blew on his hands and looked over his shoulder. "Where to?"

"The Palmer House, please," Miss Ritz said.

"That's a busy place Sunday afternoons," the cabbie said. "Folks need to make reservations a week out at least."

Miss Ritz didn't respond.

"Hope you got yourselves a reservation."

"We do."

Without another word, the cabbie pulled away from the curb and headed toward Kedzie Avenue. Gazing out the window, I looked up at the gray sky. My buttoned-up thoughts slipped out a bit. Could there be a family waiting for me at the Palmer House? Had Miss Ritz planned it this way all along? If not, when did Miss Ritz make a reservation? No. I didn't care, and I wouldn't think about any of it.

With my mind blank and only the dreary city to look at, it seemed like forever before the cabbie called out, "Here we are."

Inside the Palmer House, there was nothing dreary. My first thought confirmed that Noreen had been right; there is gold paint. It was everywhere. I'd never seen a such a high ceiling all covered with fancy arches and gold curlicues. Hundreds of lights dazzled all over the walls, on amazing lamp stands, and hanging from the ceiling. I followed Miss Ritz through the crowd of people, wearing thick fur coats, gleaming jewels, and hats with swooping feathers. Holding the polished brass banister, we climbed wide, plush-carpet stairs through a curtained doorway to a carved wooden podium.

Miss Ritz pulled off her gloves and leaned to whisper something to a tall thin man with a very pointy nose. He nodded toward the row of men standing behind him wearing short white jackets, black bow ties, and black trousers with a knife edge crease. Picking up two black leather folders, the first man in line led Miss Ritz and me to one of the many tables covered in sleek white cloths. He slipped out one of the chairs for Miss Ritz, and, when she was seated, he slid out the other one.

I stared at him.

"Your seat, miss."

Embarrassed, I sat. There were so many fancy things on the table I counted them. Four sparkling glasses with stems. Six pieces of silverware. Three white plates with gold edges stacked by size. Two gold-edged cups with gold-edged saucers. One smaller than the other. Busy with my counting, I didn't notice the man in the white jacket patiently waiting with a black folder held out to me.

"My name is Edouard," he said when I took it and then he picked up something folded like a crown. With a flick of his wrist he shook it out and laid it on my lap. A napkin. "I will give you a few moments," Edouard said before disappearing into the splendor.

The folder was huge and smelled of real leather. "What do I do with this?" I asked.

"That's your menu, dear," Miss Ritz said. "Choose whatever you'd like."

Men in black and white bustled around the dining room, each with a white cloth draped over one arm and a gleaming metal pitcher. Maybe the cloth was one of the napkins that covered my entire lap and then some. Arriving at our table, one of them held the pitcher against the napkin and poured water with tiny ice cubes into the tallest glasses.

"Please close your mouth, Debbie," Miss Ritz whispered.

"Sorry." A laughy noise escaped my lips.

I opened the folder and began reading through the menu items. Under *Appetizers,* I found Blue points, Cherrystones, and Rockaways. I pressed my lips tight to keep from shouting, "Is this food?"

"Why don't you select something from the dinners," Miss Ritz said.

"Four dollars? Each?" I blurted out much too loud.

"That is not a surprise to me," Miss Ritz said in a quiet voice. "Please order anything."

Cold soup; chopped chicken livers; oysters? How could I eat any of that? Then I saw Roast Young Tom Turkey. No, I should have something I'd never heard of before.

When Edouard returned, Miss Ritz ordered almond encrusted perch, a salad, and a baked potato with sour cream and chives. I pointed at a choice that I couldn't pronounce.

"Fricassee of Spring Chicken Jardinière," Edouard said. "Excellent choice. Would you like a salad with that?"

I nodded and added, "May I have sweetbreads, too." Edward looked at Miss Ritz who shook her head. The waiter smiled and without a word left the table.

"Dinner rolls are complimentary," Miss Ritz said. "And—sweetbreads are actually edible glands of an animal, most likely lamb."

"Oh," I said my face getting hot. I stared at a silver dish sitting in the middle of the table with carved yellow balls that looked like roses. Was it butter? Here it was impossible to be sure.

Miss Ritz reached for her glass of water. "I've realized I might have saved you from another embarrassment today, and I want to apologize."

My heart stopped. Everything was so amazing, I hadn't thought of why I was here since we arrived.

"I should have explained before this afternoon," Miss Ritz took a sip of water. "But I'd planned to tell you when we were here alone. To make it easier for you."

Easier? I blinked slowly pulling in a deep breath during the long moment my eyes were closed. Opening them, I tried to rearrange my face to keep it from giving away my feelings. The look on Miss Ritz's face made it seem like it would be okay to listen.

"Your case is unique to us at The Home. We normally do not take in children who have any . . . living family. In the rare cases where children do have family, they are usually . . . " Miss Ritz paused as if looking for the right words. " . . . unavailable to care for their children."

"What does that mean?" My words came out sounding rude. Had my mother been unavailable?

"Sometimes children have parents who are," Miss Ritz glanced around and spoke in a softer voice, "institutionalized or imprisoned. But that has been the case only once or twice. Most of our children are orphans."

I didn't want to think of anyone having a parent in prison, but I did remember Dawn. Her dad didn't come home from the war either, and her mom had tuberculosis and had to go to a sanatorium. She'd been my best friend the first two months I was at The Home, but her mom got better, and Dawn left. "I remember Dawn Anderson," I said. "She went home with her mom the day before Mary Ellen came."

"That's correct. But, for you . . ." Miss Ritz paused again. "You may not repeat what I am about to tell you. In fact, I was told not to tell you. But I believe you are old enough and that you should know." She took a deep breath. "Your Uncle Lloyd is a good friend of one of our board members. He requested we take you when your grandmother passed. Because . . . because your mother couldn't manage without your grandmother. And, well, your case has a lot of extenuating circumstances."

Miss Ritz smiled, but her eyes looked sad.

Confused, I asked, "So, that's why no one wanted me? Because of my extenuating circumstances?"

"No, no. It isn't that no one wanted you. Not at all." Miss Ritz reached across all the plates and silverware and took my hand in hers. "When I interviewed the couples who came this afternoon, if they were interested in a girl your age, I had to tell them, you, the pretty, dark-haired girl in the shiny blue dress were not available."

My thoughts swirled. Pretty? Not available? The shiny dress? It was as if my favorite dress had betrayed me. But, no, it was only a dress that anyone would notice. "So, do I have to live at The Home until—"

I jerked my hand away from hers. "Until I graduate from high school? And, what then? You'll give me a job helping Mrs. Bell?"

"No, that's not it at all." Miss Ritz sat up her straightest. "It looks like I have made a mistake. I should not have told you all of this, I—"

Edouard interrupted our conversation, placing a bowl of salad in front of each of us. Holding out a long, narrow, piece of carved wood, he said, "Pepper?"

"Yes, please." Miss Ritz smiled as if we'd been discussing a lovely book we both recently read. But I didn't miss the death grip she had on her fork.

Shaking my head, I did not look up at Edouard. "No, thank you."

After taking a bite, chewing, and swallowing, Miss Ritz cleared her throat in a very ladylike way and said, "Once again, I am sorry. I have said too much. But I assure you, your idea of your future is not accurate. And that is all I can say." Miss Ritz took another slow bite. "Now, how do you like your salad?"

Salad? Miss Ritz might as well have slapped brown wrapping tape across my mouth. I pulled in all my thoughts and feelings buttoning them up even tighter than before. Then lifting my chin, I stared across the room. Gram's ideas about respecting adults somehow slipped into my head. I focused on the things Gram had taught me and said, "I don't know as I've ever had a salad before." And silently I prayed, *Dear God in Heaven, please help me to behave like I should. And please, please, help me to believe You are in control of everything.*

On the way back to The Home, a different cabbie proved to be smarter than our first one. When he didn't get a response to his comment on the slushy streets, he stopped trying to talk to us. There was no point in talking to Miss Ritz anyway. I understood that, but I sure as blazes didn't like it. Why did adults act like a girl's future was none of her own business? Didn't Miss Ritz care how it felt to never know what was going to happen next? She said she did, but, clearly, she didn't.

Back at The Home, the silence inside made it clear none of the other children had returned yet. I put one foot in front of the other and began climbing the stairs.

Miss Ritz cleared her throat.

Hope surged into every part of me. Miss Ritz must be ready to say whatever she wouldn't tell me at dinner. I stopped and turned, my heart thumping wildly.

With one hand on the newel post, Miss Ritz raised her eyebrows and asked, "Did you forget something?"

Had I forgotten something? So much had happened that whole afternoon and evening, everything blurred together. What could I be forgetting?

"A thank you," she said.

"Oh. Um . . . sorry, thank you." Before the words could choke me, before the "thank you" could make me burst into tears, I stormed up the stairs. Running through the empty dorm, I banged open the door to the Big Girls' Room and slammed it shut. Flinging myself onto my bed I unbuttoned the thoughts that had built into an entire mountain of hurts.

Sobbing. Exhausted. Alone. I slipped into a deep sleep.

CHAPTER THIRTY

UNTOLD

"Are you awake, Debbie?"

"Let her sleep."

Repeated poking on my back made me roll over and squint my eyes open to see the poker. Sharon.

"You are awake! Did you have fun? Where did you go? Who picked you?" Sharon's questions came so fast I couldn't think of any answers. Of course, that didn't matter one smidgen to Sharon. "I had a marvelous time," she said. "Phillip and Margie took me to Wimpy's. In case you didn't know, Wimpy's is the hippest hamburger joint around."

Clearly horrified, Noreen actually interrupted. "You didn't really call them by their first names, did you?"

"They told me to, don't ya know." Sharon stood in the middle of the room and stretched.

Noreen frowned. "If someone told you to jump off the Empire State building, would you do it?"

I buried my face in my pillow. What could I say to them? I didn't want to lie, but I couldn't bring myself to tell the truth.

"Well, Paul and I had a wonderful time, too. With Mr. and Mrs. Sullivan and their whole family. Who did pick you, Debbie?"

"A single woman took me out," I said sitting up on the edge of my bed.

"Really?" Sharon asked. "Miss Ritz pulled the old switcheroo and let you go out with a single woman? But I thought—"

"She took me to The Palmer House," I said in a rush. "I can hardly describe how amazing it is. The ceilings must be twenty feet high, maybe thirty. And they have these unbelievable pictures painted on them, all surrounded by gold curlicues."

"Lucky duck." Sharon jumped in when I took a breath. "Like I was saying, Phillip and Margie took me to Wimpy's because everyone knows Wimpy's is first rate, and we wanted to have time to take in a movie, too."

"What did you see?" I asked hoping to keep her talking.

"Oh, dah-ling," Sharon said in a haughty dramatic voice I'd never heard her use before. "*Auntie Mame*, of course. It was so mah-velous, simply mah-velous!" Her voice went back to normal. "I want to be exactly like Mamie. She takes in her orphaned nephew, Patrick. He's such a cutie. She teaches him how to live, live, live. When Patrick grows up, he's so so handsome. And, Miss Agnes Gooch is hilarious; even when she gets pregnant, we just died laughing at her. Phillip said she plain fractured him."

"Did you say *Miss* Agnes Gooch?" Noreen asked. "That does not sound appropriate." She turned her back to the room, pulled off her nightgown, and put on her dress.

"Don't be such a fuddy-duddy." Sharon pulled on her skirt. "It was only a movie, don't ya know."

"What did you do, Noreen?" I asked turning away to put on my dress and to dodge any more questions.

"Mrs. Sullivan roasted two chickens with all the trimmings. We sat and talked at the table for hours. It was easy to be with them. And fun."

"How about you and this single woman?" Sharon asked.

"I had chicken, too. But it was called 'Fricassee of Spring Chicken Jardinière', which was really just a fancy name for chicken with no bones. It's a wonder how they do that, take out the bones and still leave the pieces full size. Plus, the vegetables were cut into tiny pieces and it had gravy drizzled over all of it. It looked so beautiful that I could barely bring myself to eat it."

I swallowed the memory of pushing the food around my plate without taking a single bite. I'd been sure it would never go down my throat after all the things Miss Ritz had said. But, mostly because of the things she didn't.

Sharon kept going on and on about the "mah-velous" time she had. I did my best to look busy getting dressed, and I could tell Noreen was ever so much better and that made me happy.

On the way down to breakfast, everyone was whispering about the outing. It sounded like they all had a wonderful time, making me decide to be happy for them and forget my experience. For the next two days, I was able to dodge Sharon's nosy questions and Noreen's sincere curiosity.

When Sunday rolled around, everyone was reminded of the outing. The old gray couple picked up Mary Ellen. Tommy and two other boys went out with their couples again. As did Diane. Nancy and her two little brothers were all picked up by the couple who had taken Nancy for the outing, which caused a bit of a stir. Surely the three of them and the others were headed for adoption.

I told myself I didn't care about any of it. I forced myself to forget the whole outing by rereading *Miracles on Maple Hill*. The book had turned out differently than I'd expected, but I still loved it. Whenever I looked at the picture on the cover of Marly in that nice red coat, I just knew she had parents who loved her.

Even reading couldn't stop me from thinking of Mary Ellen. She'd told me the old couple, Mr. and Mrs. Murphy, were so very nice. They'd taken her shopping and let her buy anything she wanted from Marshall Field's. She'd chosen a doll with long brown curls and a blue dress.

"Mrs. Murphy said they'll keep her for me. She said they'll bring her back to visit me on Sundays." Mary Ellen searched my eyes for approval. "I named her Elizabeth Anne. I hope you don't mind."

"That was my favorite doll's name," I said.

"I know." Mary Ellen hurried on to explain. "At first, I named her Kathleen Anne just like my favorite doll. But Mrs. Murphy pulled a hanky out of her pocketbook." Mary Ellen pressed her lips tight and put her fist against them. "She did this. So, I knew that name wasn't a good idea. The only other name I could think of right away was Elizabeth Anne."

"It was very thoughtful of you to notice how Mrs. Murphy felt."

Mary Ellen smiled and ducked her head. "Then we went to Cozy Corner Restaurant. That's their favorite. On the way in, Mr. Murphy whispered that their son's daughter Kathleen was . . . you know, in that fire."

Mary Ellen looked so sad, I patted her arm. "Elizabeth Anne is the perfect name. Thank you for using it."

After Mary Ellen and the others left, I wandered into the game room and stared at the wooden cradle. Someone had put two dolls in it side by side. An old Shirley Temple with almost no hair left and the ugliest doll there, the one with a plastic painted head, no moving parts and a dirty-yellow, plaid-cloth body. As I thought about sitting in the parlor all by myself after everyone left, I felt like that doll. It made me glad someone put her in the cradle with the famous Shirley.

Seeing those dolls made me think of how pretty the new Elizabeth Anne must be. Maybe I was wrong. Maybe a home with Mr. and Mrs. Murphy would be better for Mary Ellen.

I was so confused. But, somehow, I had hope that everything would work out after all. Maybe it was because Miss Ritz took me out and almost did tell me what was in store for me. And, she said my future wasn't what I thought. Or, maybe it was because Gram always told me to trust God because He knew exactly how things would end up. So, for now, I made up my mind that was enough for me.

CHAPTER THIRTY-ONE

UNEASY

Patricia leaned over our breakfast table on Sunday morning. "Miss Ritz wants to see you before church."

As soon as we got to the Big Girls' Room, Sharon closed the door. "What did Patricia tell you?"

"Miss Ritz wants to talk to me."

Sharon's eyes got big and she drew in a breath making a silent 'o' with her mouth.

"Sharon, stop that," Noreen said. She patted my arm. "I'm sure it will be fine."

Even though I knew Noreen meant well, none of us had any idea why Miss Ritz wanted to talk to me. Would she finish telling me about my future? Or worse, did she have bad news for me? I prayed all the way to the office.

Miss Ritz sat tall behind her desk looking like she expected me to be delighted. "Your Uncle Lloyd called."

I held my breath. What now?

"He and your mother will be picking you up for Sunday dinner. When you get back from church, you can wait for them in here," Miss Ritz said. "Instead of waiting in the front parlor with the other children getting picked up. Since this is . . . a different kind of circumstance, I thought you might like some privacy."

My thoughts ran off to places they'd never dared to go before whirling out of control. All the way back up the stairs I tried to figure out what was going on. I'd been here since the day after my birthday seven months ago. What made today special? Did my mother really want to see me? Would she be sober? Would Uncle Lloyd be mean or nice? Why couldn't they just leave me alone? I was used to that.

Grabbing the banister to keep my balance, I let out a cold laugh, "Ha." It figured. First, they ignore me, and now, they come here to embarrass me over and over. How would I ever stand it?

Before I knew it, and way before I was ready, we were back from church and I was sitting with Miss Ritz in her office. I sat in front of her desk, while she concentrated on some papers in a folder. Were they about me?

Getting warmer and warmer in my ugly brown coat, I wished I'd taken it off before I sat down. I didn't want to do it now and have Miss Ritz look up at me. I didn't think I'd like to see what her eyes would say.

My insides were so jumpy I had to focus on swinging my feet in even circles to keep the rest of myself still. The thought of what Mr. Kelly would say to that sort of sitting still came to mind but thinking of him would only make this wait worse. So much worse. This was not the time to think of school, but I could think about the concert and my solo. I couldn't imagine what to hope for, but I liked knowing I could hope.

At the sound of the front door opening, my brain froze. I adjusted my face wishing I could wipe off every shred of emotion, folded my hands in my lap, and studied them. Listening to the footsteps, light tappy heels, along with heavy thundery wingtips, I sat up straighter and pulled in a deep breath.

The footsteps stopped.

A long awkward silence filled the room.

I licked my lips without moving.

Miss Ritz cleared her throat. I ignored her.

"Hello, Debbie." My mother's voice.

No slurring.

Breathing slowly, I turned to the door with all my emotions wiped off my face.

She stood in the office doorway holding a package tied up with curly blue ribbon.

I could barely believe it.

It was my mother.

Not my drunk mother.

But, Mom.

The way she used to be, and Uncle Lloyd behind her with his hat in his hands. Smiling.

I eyed the package.

No one moved.

Holding out the gift, Mom smiled with so much hope and so much love, I didn't know what to think. I couldn't handle all the feelings rushing around in my head. And my heart. And even my shaky hands. I had to button them up inside.

"A present." Miss Ritz's voice rang out in the silence. "Open it, Debbie. Let's see what it is."

Still, no one moved.

Miss Ritz got up and took the gift from Mom. "Very thoughtful," she said setting it on my lap right on top of my hands.

The box was at least twice as big as my lap. Under the blue ribbon, it was wrapped in birthday paper.

"It's not my birthday," I said. I kept my heart far, far away from my words.

"I know that," Mom said. "But I missed your birthday—" Her voice squeezed tight. "I don't know how any mother could do such a thing . . ." Her voice trailed off.

I couldn't say anything, so I stared at the gift. There were pictures of girls in blue dresses and blue skirts. And a girl in a pink dress sitting in a blue chair. In between the girls, the words "Happy Birthday" were written over and over and over. I studied the details trying not to think or feel anything until the box started to slide off my lap.

I grabbed it.

Without saying a word, without looking up, I began to slowly tear the paper off the box. Under the paper, the box was green with *Marshall Field's* written in white cursive letters across the top. Feeling like I was watching someone else's hands, I lifted the top off revealing layers of pure white tissue. Hands that didn't feel like mine pushed the tissue aside.

A gasp burst out of me.

The image of a girl leaning against a tree on the front of my favorite book, a girl who was loved, filled my thoughts unbuttoning all my hurt and disappointment and confusion.

Nestled in all that tissue, lay a brand-spanking new coat. A dark blue, tweed coat with wooden buttons. Buttons that were attached in a row down the front with heavy cord. Each one across from a heavy cord loop for the buttonhole. Lifting the coat, I buried my face in it.

Unwanted

In that moment, my wounded thoughts and disappointments and determined anger were defeated by the simple . . .

beautiful . . .

blue . . .

coat.

"How did you know?" I whispered.

CHAPTER THIRTY-TWO

UNLOVABLE

Going out to Sunday dinner with Mom and Uncle Lloyd felt like it was happening to someone else. Like a television show where everyone is happy by the end of the program, but you know it's not real. Mom sat right next to me in the back seat of Uncle Lloyd's car.

"What am I, the chauffeur?" Uncle Lloyd asked clearly pretending to complain.

"Of course you are," Mom teased back. "Where would you like to dine, my dear?" she asked me in a silly haughty voice.

I didn't know what to say. I didn't know how to relax. What if this was the last time I saw them for another seven months?

"How about Cozy Corner," Uncle Lloyd said. "It's right up on Diversey."

That was the restaurant Mary Ellen had gone to with the Murphys so I nodded.

"Splendid. Please take us there immediately," Mom said in the same silly voice. "But, do drive carefully."

Uncle Lloyd laughed.

As soon as he pulled away from the curb, Mom turned and took both of my hands in hers. "I know I can't change the past," she said her eyes shiny with tears. "I so wish I could, but I can't. I do know what I can do. I can do better today and every day from now on."

What could I say to that?

Nothing.

"I don't want to make any excuses," Mom said. "Because nothing excuses some of the choices I've made. I'm not blaming anyone, but myself. After . . . Uncle Lloyd took you to—" Mom stopped and looked over my shoulder for a moment. Like she was trying to hold on to her emotions before she went on.

"I got worse for a while. Much worse. I didn't want to think of all the sad things that had happened in my life so I drank to forget, and it worked. I forgot everything. But it made me forget things I didn't want to forget, too. Now, I am truly sorry for that time in my life."

Mom took a deep breath. I could hear it shake in her chest.

"I thought of you every day, and I'd try to stop drinking. But then, I'd feel so disgusted with myself and helpless that I'd take just one drink and feel like such a failure that I'd feel even sadder. So, I'd have another. It took a long time to recognize the downward spiral I was stuck in."

Her words slipped in and out of my brain without touching my heart.

"I knew I had to stop drinking and was sure I could do it by myself. I tried stopping so many times, I lost count. Sadly, it took me way too long to see that I would never be able to do it. Finally, Uncle Lloyd convinced me that I needed God's help. So, I started to pray . . . like Gram taught me. For the first time in a long time, I went for a whole week without one drop."

Why was Mom telling me all this?

"I knew about AA, *Alcoholics Anonymous,* but I was too embarrassed and ashamed to try it. Until Christmas Eve." Mom pressed her lips together and stared out the window.

"On Christmas Eve, I went to a party with an old friend," Mom said. "As soon as I got there, I knew I should go home, but it was Christmas Eve, so I didn't. And, as you know, I fell off the wagon."

Her voice was almost too quiet it to hear. Or, maybe I just didn't want to hear it. I wanted her to stop saying "Christmas Eve." With my jaw clenched tight holding in all my words—mean, hurtful words—I stared over her head.

"I promise. I will never do anything like that again," Mom said squeezing both my hands. "I don't blame you at all if you don't believe me, but I will keep that promise. And I intend to do everything I can to prove it to you."

One lonely tear spilled down her cheek.

"When I woke up on Christmas day it was the worst day of my life," Mom said talking faster as if she had to get the whole story out right away. "I prayed like I've never prayed before. I knew God would help me, but I had to help myself too. Uncle Lloyd found an AA meeting and dropped me off. There were a lot of people there. When it was my turn to stand up and speak, I told everyone, 'My name is Carol Spencer. I am an alcoholic, and I cannot ever hurt my daughter again like I did yesterday.' That's the day I met Arlene, my sponsor. I've gone to over thirty meetings in the last eight and half weeks. I've talked to Arlene on the phone every day and I've met with her when I didn't have a meeting. I keep going back because I know it's what God wants me to do. But, mostly, it's because of you."

Tears welled up in my eyes. I blinked to hold them in.

"Arlene keeps encouraging me. She's the best friend I'll ever have."

I couldn't look at her, so I kept my eyes on our hands. They were like a bridge connecting us to each other. I wanted to believe her, but I couldn't. Not yet anyway.

Mom touched my cheek. "Just wait and see," she said.

A few minutes later, Uncle Lloyd pulled into a parking space in front of the restaurant. "We're here," he said. "And that's enough talking about the past, okay?"

"I need Debbie to know." Mom turned to the window. "I'll never forgive myself."

"Now Carol," Uncle Lloyd said. "You gotta stop beating yourself up because of all that. A lot of the blame belongs to that dame at your office, what's her name, Shirley, she's the one that insisted one little drink wouldn't hurt."

"But I should have known better."

"From now on you'll know what to do. Focus on the future," Uncle Lloyd said. "You still haven't told Debbie any good news. This is supposed to be a celebration, right Squirt?" He eyed me in the rear-view mirror wiggling his eyebrows the same way Doris always did to make me laugh. I managed a smile.

In the restaurant, Uncle Lloyd suggested I order a veal cutlet with mashed potatoes and gravy and peas and carrots.

"Tell her something good, Carol," Uncle Lloyd said to Mom.

"Okay." Mom caught my eyes with hers. Her eyes told me she meant everything she said. Even her promise. I knew my eyes weren't telling her anything.

"Well, I got a job. I am a secretary for an insurance company downtown. Uncle Lloyd still repairs houses but works for himself now. Plus, we've been going to church every Sunday, and I joined the choir."

I couldn't think of what to say. And I wasn't ready to say anything. Mom went on like she understood.

"Well now," Mom said. "I have choir practice on Wednesday nights. I'm going to attend AA meetings every Tuesday, Thursday, and Saturday night. Tell her about bowling, Lloyd."

"I joined a bowling team." Uncle Lloyd scooped up an enormous bite of his veal cutlet after covering it in mashed potatoes. "Friday nights," he said before shoveling the bite into his mouth.

"Last week, Arlene and I went along to watch," Mom said. "I can't wait for Arlene to meet you."

"Arlene says all your mother talks about is you," Uncle Lloyd said. "She must think I'm too boring to mention."

"She knows better than that," Mom said. "She's seen you with your bowling team."

Uncle Lloyd laughed. Looking at my plate he said, "You'd better eat up before your food gets cold. I'm planning to eat anything you can't finish, and I prefer my food warm."

I almost smiled at that. It seemed like Uncle Lloyd was a funny guy after all. Now.

Mom and Uncle Lloyd joked with each other about bowling and his dirty socks in the living room and lots of other things for the rest of our meal. We stopped at the bowling alley, but all the lanes were full, so we headed back to The Home. Both of them walked me in.

Patricia jumped up from the davenport in the parlor. "Miss Ritz asked me to check everyone in. Did you have a nice time?"

"Sure did," Uncle Lloyd answered for all of us. Did he wink at Patricia?

Patricia relaxed when she saw my smile.

"We want to pick up Debbie every Sunday," Mom said.

"Okay," Patricia said. "I'll tell Miss Ritz."

Mom took both my hands in hers again. "I love you, Debbie. We'll see you next week." She squeezed my hands and turned to hurry out.

"Next week, kiddo," Uncle Lloyd said following right behind her.

I smiled. But I knew my eyes were afraid to smile just in case that never happened.

Before the big front door clicked shut, I grabbed the stair railing and started plodding up to the Big Girls' Room. My thoughts and feelings ran every which way like they were in a maze with all dead ends.

"Debbie," Patricia said. "Did you forget your new coat? You left it in the office."

Stopping mid-step, I couldn't think how to answer

"Do you want to put it on and wear it upstairs?" Patricia asked.

I shook my head.

"I understand," Patricia said. "Everyone will want to know where you got such a beautiful coat and I imagine that might be more than you want to talk about just yet."

I nodded.

"Would you like me to bring it up when all of you come down to watch television?" Patricia said. "I could put it in your drawer."

"Thanks," I said. "Our bottom one is empty."

"You can take it out when you're ready." Patricia put her hand on my arm. "You've had a lot to handle today."

With a small smile, I headed straight to the Big Girls' Room. As I stepped in, Noreen looked up from praying. Sharon glanced at me with a smile and her hand under her pillow probably holding her paperback.

"Wherever have you been?" Sharon asked.

"Sharon!" Noreen said. "Maybe it's private."

"It is, kind of," I said. I scrambled to think of what to say. I didn't want to talk about all the things my mother said in the car. "My mother and my uncle took me out for dinner."

"Really?" Sharon's mouth dropped open. She didn't even try to hide her shock and curiosity.

Noreen was better about it. "That's nice."

"It was," I said wishing I could just keep it all to myself. But I knew Noreen really cared for me, and I supposed Sharon did, too. Maybe they deserved to know. "Please don't say anything to anyone else," I said looking right at Sharon.

"Cross my heart and hope to die," Sharon said crossing her heart with one finger and then pretending to stick a needle in her eye.

"Of course not," Noreen said.

Pulling a breath in through my nose, I spoke it as fast as I could. "My mother stopped drinking and she's really sorry."

"Forgive and forget," Noreen said. "Isn't that what the Bible says?"

Sharon nodded. She pulled out her paperback, but I saw her looking at me over the top of it like she didn't know what to think. Mrs. Petersen's bell called us to line up, and we all filed into the parlor to watch *Lassie*. The whole time it seemed like I was watching myself do all the Sunday night things. Even when Mary Ellen told me what fun she had with the Murphys and Elizabeth Anne, I smiled and said I was so glad. But I didn't feel like myself.

CHAPTER THIRTY-THREE

UNEXPECTED

At school the next day, every time I thought of going out with my mother and Uncle Lloyd, I made myself stop. I couldn't think about it at school, and I couldn't tell Doris either. Not yet. So, after school, when we got to the Spaulding corner, I decided to tell Doris what I'd been thinking about Roberta instead. Up until then, Doris had been excited about the concert practice and Miss Bailey being fair and all that I didn't try to get a word in edgewise.

"What did you think of Roberta's idea to use the word hope?" I asked.

Doris stopped with her mouth open, "I'm not sure."

"That's exactly what I've been thinking," I said. "I mean there's no doubt Roberta isn't nice, and Mr. Kelly thinks she's the best."

"And, I think she likes to get you in trouble," Doris said.

"True," I said. "But, her new words for that song were good."

"Okay," Doris said. "I'll admit that, but you know she's going to think she's a real poet now."

"Maybe," I said. "I have to admit when I stopped thinking about who thought of those words and just sang them, they fit perfectly."

Doris looked puzzled.

"Singing them made me wonder if maybe Roberta does have to pretend life is wonderful sometimes," I said. "How would she think that up if it wasn't real. And, I thought maybe she's just like any other girl. Like us."

"Not quite," Doris said. "She's spoiled, and we're not."

"Right, but she didn't pick her family any more than you or I did."

"I know you're probably right," Doris said. "But I need to think about this."

"Me too," I said. "And I think we need to pray about it."

Doris let out a huge sigh. "Okay, okay. I'll try to be nice to your new best friend." She laughed and took off running towards home.

As soon as Doris left, Mary Ellen blurted out, "I've got a solo for the Easter Concert."

"Is that so?" I asked.

"Uh huh," Mary Ellen said. "The first and second grades are singing "Peter Cottontail" together. Miss Bailey brought in a record, and we all listened to Gene Autry singing it. After the song, she wants us to recite three poems: one for winter, one for spring, and one for summer. I get to say part of the winter one, 'Bushes look like popcorn balls'."

"That's wonderful. You said it so nice and slow," I said. "And loud."

Mary Ellen grinned. "Wait. No. That's not right. It's supposed to be 'The bushes' How will I ever remember to say every word just right. It makes a difference for a poem, Miss Bailey said so."

"Don't worry, I'll help you practice, and, at the concert, I'm positive you'll do it perfectly."

For the rest of the week, all I thought of was the Easter concert. I would not let myself think about my mother or Uncle Lloyd. I couldn't stand it if they didn't show up next Sunday, and I didn't know how I'd feel if they did. On Sunday morning, Patricia came up to me as soon as I got to my seat in the dining hall for breakfast.

"I have a message for you," she said with a smile.

Despite the smile, I held my breath waiting to hear what it was.

"Your uncle called. They will be here right after breakfast. They want to take you to their church so you're to wait for them in the parlor. I'll be there to check you out."

After that, I couldn't even remember what I ate for breakfast. In the parlor, Patricia had something dark blue over her arm, before I had time to figure out what, she held up my new coat.

"I'm sorry I didn't ask first," she said in a hurry. "But, there really wasn't an opportunity. I wanted to get it while you were at breakfast. I thought you'd want to have it on when they got here; that way your mom will know you're grateful."

"I am grateful," I said. When I decided not to run up to the Big Girls' Room to get it, I hadn't thought of that. "I guess I should wear it."

"If you want, I can put it in your drawer discreetly after you get back," Patricia said. "I guess I'm assuming you had a good time last Sunday."

Ever since the night she'd taken care of me in the Infirmary, I felt closer to Patricia like I could tell her things I would never tell anyone else. "I did," I said. "My mother filled me in on all the things that happened with her while I was here."

Patricia nodded.

"A lot of it was downright awful, but I'm pretty sure she's going to . . . well, you know, do what's right."

"You mean not drinking."

"Yes." I guess Patricia felt comfortable talking to me, too. "It's hard for me to talk about it. Maybe that's silly, but it is. I hardly talked at all when I was out with them last week."

"Really," Patricia said. "I find that hard to believe." She laughed. But then she got serious and said, "I understand feeling awkward talking about alcoholism. That's how I ended up here. Both my parents died because of it."

"I'm so sorry," I said.

"I am, too. But that was a long time ago, and things are looking up for me these days," Patricia smiled. She turned a bit pink in the face and hurried to the door. "Look," she said. "Here they are now."

Uncle Lloyd held the door open for Mom. He smiled at Patricia and, when she blushed, so did he. That was odd. Mom didn't seem to notice so I didn't say anything. It still felt like the three of us were strangers. Patricia had Mom sign a form, and we headed off to church.

I loved going back to the church I'd known for as long as I could remember before I came to The Home. It was more lively and the pastor seemed happy sharing the Bible with everyone. Mom sat with the choir next to the platform in front, which gave me the opportunity to watch her during the whole service. Being in church and watching how sincere she seemed made me feel more connected to her. Afterward, Uncle Lloyd surprised both of us by heading to the Walnut Room at Marshall Field's for dinner.

"I couldn't get reservations last week," he said.

Mom turned to look at me in the back seat. "I heard your voice all the way up in the choir loft this morning," she said. "Debbie, you sing beautifully."

"I'll say," Uncle Lloyd agreed. "Sounds exactly like you, Carol."

"Would you come to church with us every Sunday?" Mom asked.

I'd been wondering how Mary Ellen made it to church without me. So, I didn't know how to answer without hurting Mom's feelings.

"Please tell me how you really feel," Mom said.

I fiddled with one of the wooden buttons on my new coat.

"I know you walk to church," Mom said. "Is that a time you get to talk to friends, too."

"It is," I said. "But, it's mostly because, on the way to church, I always watch out for a little girl. She's the youngest girl at The Home and my favorite." I didn't tell Mom that I pretend she's my little sister. "I really do like your church so much better. But once, Mary Ellen, that's her name, fell and . . . "

Mom's eyes filled up quickly. "You are such a nice girl," she said. "Maybe, for now, we can pick you up right after you get back from church."

"Thanks, I'd like that," I said looking right at her.

Clearly, Mom knew how eyes could talk.

"For now," I added to be sure she understood.

Before going into the Walnut Room, we stopped at the coat room. Uncle Lloyd helped Mom take her coat off and handed it over the half door to the attendant. He reached to help me, but I pulled back. "Oh no, I'll keep my coat with me."

Uncle Lloyd laughed. "It'll be here when we're done." He helped me slip it off.

Watching the attendant take my beautiful coat, I prayed Uncle Lloyd was right. I hadn't even worn it to school yet because I didn't want to be a showoff or explain where I got it and it might get wet and dirty.

Marshall Field's Walnut Room was almost as fabulous as the Palmer House, but I did not say so out loud. I felt a bit proud that I already knew about luxury dining.

After studying the menu, Uncle Lloyd announced, "I'll have Swiss steak with pan gravy and whipped potatoes. Care to join me, Debbie? Potatoes whipped to within an inch of their lives are even better than mashed."

It turned out he was right, the potatoes almost melted in my mouth. When we were done eating, Uncle Lloyd said, "I suppose you gals want to do a little shopping since we're here. I guess I don't mind tagging along."

Uncle Lloyd got up and pulled Mom's chair out for her and then mine. It did seem like he was different. Mom sure was. She didn't have a hair out of place. Her green dress had subtle lighter green polka dots, three-quarter length sleeves, and, with a pretty dangling bow tied at her neck, simple but elegant. We got on the elevator where a lady in a uniform pulled the door closed and turned a lever next to door which made the elevator go up. When the elevator came to a stop, the operator opened the door and called out, "second floor women's dresses, women's shoes." At the next stop, "third floor, children's clothing, children's shoes, toys."

Mom stepped out with a smile.

I hoped she wasn't planning to buy anything for me.

"Let's go look at the dresses," Mom said. "They have such lovely things here."

"Thanks, Mom. But, at The Home we all share the clothes," I said.

Mom gave Uncle Lloyd a look that seemed to say, "I am the worst mother in the world."

"It's all right," I said. "If we didn't, some girls might have better clothes than others. That wouldn't be fair."

Mom turned away.

"How about the toy department?" Uncle Lloyd asked.

I shook my head. I didn't want to say anything else that could make Mom feel worse.

"There's a news stand around the corner," Uncle Lloyd said. "I'll bet you'd like a comic book."

"That would be nice," I said. "But you don't have to buy me anything. Just going out is really fun."

I could see Mom was upset.

When they dropped me off at The Home later, Mom took both my hands in hers, again. I knew she had something important to say.

"I want you to know," Mom said. "When I hear about all the things you've missed because of living here instead of in a real home, it makes me sad. It makes me more determined to stay sober, too."

I squeezed her hands.

"I can see," she said. "Instead of having a chip on your shoulder you've learned to be kind and generous and thoughtful. I am proud of you."

Maybe now I could be proud of her, too. I hoped so.

CHAPTER THIRTY-FOUR

UNRIVALED

The next morning, I pulled my beautiful blue coat out of the bottom drawer. Since I got it back unharmed at Marshall Field's, it seemed like a shame to keep it hidden.

"What a beautiful coat," Noreen said.

"Thanks," I said. "It's from my mom."

"Splendiferous." Sharon saluted. "Love those buttons and loops, too."

When I gave Mrs. Petersen the ugly brown one, she said, "Your new coat is beautiful. I'll put this old one away in case another girl has a need for it someday."

At school, Doris couldn't stop grinning at me. "That is one gorgeous coat, and it's almost the same color as mine."

I told her it was a gift from my mom and almost sighed with relief when she didn't ask any questions. Each compliment for my wonderful coat felt like a message of love from Mom.

Leaving school a few days later, lazy flakes of snow wafted from a heavy-white sky. As they floated to the ground, I could almost count the points on each one. I spotted Mary Ellen at the Maple. "Snow," she yelled. Twirling with her arms up to the sky and her head back, she stuck her tongue out.

I copied her catching a cold flake that melted quickly. Fresh snow gave everything a layer of newness. Covering all the muckiness of the city, it left the streets, the yards, and the freshly shoveled sidewalks clean and bright. Whenever it snowed, the whole world changed.

When we got back to The Home, Mary Ellen lingered in the doorway of the Big Girls' Room. "Sing your solo for me again. Please?" She clasped her hands together at her chest. "Pretty please with sugar on top?" She gave me such a sweet hopeful look; how could I say no?

"Is anyone in the washroom?"

"Nope." Mary Ellen skipped over and held the door for me.

Leaving the door open just enough to see anyone coming, I said, "Let's both practice. You go first."

Standing tall between the rows of toilets and sinks, Mary Ellen held her hands at her sides and recited her line perfectly.

I clapped.

"It sounds really good in here," Mary Ellen said. "Now you."

I sang my solo. On the last word, "hope," I saw Nancy on the way to the washroom. "Looks like it's time for the rehearsal room to close for business," I said. "Besides, Mrs. Petersen will be ringing her bell for supper any minute now."

Skipping out the door, Mary Ellen said, "You sing really good."

I gave her a grin and held the door for Nancy.

"I agree," Nancy said.

"Thanks," I said. Every time I practiced my solo, people said that, even Miss Bailey. But still, I worried I wouldn't be able to sing it without any mistakes at the concert.

I hadn't told Mom and Uncle Lloyd about it. I knew Mom's AA meetings were on Thursday nights. I was afraid of what could happen if she skipped a meeting just to hear me sing.

When Doris asked if they were coming, I told her my other reason. "I'm not sure I can sing in front of an audience," I said. "Or if I'll remember all the words with so many people watching and listening. Mom and Uncle Lloyd don't really know much about me. I don't want them to see me as a failure."

Doris didn't ask again.

True to her word, Mom came every Sunday after church, usually with Uncle Lloyd. Except the one time he couldn't come. That time Mom had to take a bus, transfer twice, and walk from Kedzie, just to see me.

Each week, I waited for them in the front parlor with all the other kids getting picked up. More and more I felt like myself around Mom and Uncle Lloyd. By the first Sunday in March, I was excited to see them again.

As usual, Mary Ellen and I sat together on one of the davenports with Nancy at the other end. Nancy's two brothers, Wayne and Petey, raised a ruckus when they scrambled into the front parlor.

"I win," Wayne said.

"You're bigger," Petey said. "I should get a head start."

Wayne laughed. Petey went to the doorway of the foyer. "Here they come," he shouted.

"Petey," Nancy said. "You're too loud."

"Don't worry, Nan." Wayne was even louder. "I'll take care of him." He grabbed Petey, and the two went to wrestling on the floor. The couple who had come for them took one look at the boys, looked at each other, and laughed.

"I hope you're up for this every day–all day," the man said to his wife.

Laughing, she swung the door open and said much louder than most ladies, "Last one in the car is a rotten egg!" They all rushed out banging the door behind them.

Watching them run to the street, I saw Mom, Uncle Lloyd, and the Murphys meet on the sidewalk. They came in and collected Mary Ellen and me without too much noise.

"That couple adores Mary Ellen," Mom said as Uncle Lloyd held the car door open for her.

I smiled. "Isn't she cute?" Then I could feel my face get red thinking how much everyone said we look alike. I didn't want Mom to think I was vain. I just wanted Mom to like Mary Ellen.

"She's darling." Mom interrupted my thoughts before they ran too far away. She got in the front seat, and I slipped into the back.

Leaning forward, I hooked my elbow over the front bench seat and asked Mom, "Do you think they plan to adopt her?"

"They didn't mention it," Mom said. "They may be too old to adopt."

As far as I knew no one else was coming around looking to adopt little girls lately. I didn't want Mary Ellen left behind if I did get to leave The Home. But, what could I could do about it?

That night, as soon as I stepped into the dining hall, I found out I had a more urgent problem. I smelled it. Squash. I knew I was in trouble because I hated squash. Especially the way they served it at The Home. They cooked it half to death, mashed it, then heaped it into a huge bowl before one of the servers scooped it out onto everyone's plate. A nasty pile of orange mush. The worst part was everyone knew you had to eat everything on your plate no matter what.

Last time we had squash, I'd been stuck sitting at the table until after lights out. I had tried holding my nose and swallowing fast, but that never worked. My tongue did all the tasting and I couldn't get the awful stuff past it. The only reason I hadn't been there all night long was because I finally managed to wrap the mess in my napkin. Then I hid it in my pocket and flushed it down the toilet. I had stuffed the messy napkin into my coat pocket and threw it away at school. Up till now, no one had mentioned the missing napkin, but, if I kept throwing napkins in the garbage, eventually they would.

It had been months since the last squash incident, so I couldn't believe my eyes when Eileen started marching around the room slapping orange mush onto every plate. Even though my table was the last to be served, I was sure Eileen gave everyone else an extra small portion to be sure she had plenty in her bowl when she got to me.

Splat!

The orange mush landed on my plate half on top of my slice of ham. I managed to act like I didn't care by holding my breath until I had to get some air. When that smell hit my nose, I knew my whole face was saying "nasty" all on its own.

"Still don't like the squash, huh, missy?" Eileen laughed. "I'll give you more then, till you learn to love it."

Splash!

The second scoop was worse than the first. Orange mush splashed onto my favorite dress and even my arms. I held back a dry heave.

"Did I hear you say more, please?" Eileen laughed again, digging into the bowl.

Gripping the sides of my chair, I looked past my plate across the room. Paul caught my eye. He picked up a heap of squash with his spoon. Keeping his eyes on me, he held the full spoon up over his plate, pulled the top of it back with his forefinger and flung the squash across the room. It hit the side of Eileen's face with a satisfying splat and slid down into the bowl.

Eileen pulled in a loud gasp and let it out with a screech. Kids all over the room exploded into laughter shouting at each other.

"Did you see that?"

"That was a good one!"

Quicker than a wink, Miss Nielsen stood in the middle of the dining hall. She got hold of Paul's ear and dragged him out the boys' door to the golden sound of silence. A few kids pointed a finger at Paul saying, "awww," and wiping that forefinger with their other one adding, "shame on you."

During all the commotion, Sharon and Noreen scooped my squash onto their plates and scarfed it up. I sent God a thank you prayer for such good friends. Especially for Paul. He would be the best big brother ever.

CHAPTER THIRTY-FIVE

UNKNOWN

The day before St. Patrick's Day, I stepped forward for my solo at practice, and Gram's face popped into my mind. So, I sang every word as if she was sitting in the front row.

My face felt hot when everyone clapped.

"That was wonderful, Debbie." Miss Bailey stepped out from behind the piano. "All of you have improved substantially in the last ten weeks. I hope each one of you realizes how much your hard work will affect all the children in our school. The little ones are watching you, and you are a fine example for them."

The little ones. That meant Mary Ellen. She was watching me and knew something was bothering me even though I never told her how worried I was at the thought of leaving her at The Home. I knew Gram would be disappointed with all my worrying. She would say what she had said to me so many times. "Debbie, you know what God says, *'Be careful for nothing; but in every thing by prayer and supplication with thanksgiving let your requests be made known unto God'* and that means we never need to worry. We just need to trust Him."

The next day after school, Doris and Mary Ellen were waiting for me. Mary Ellen's green ribbon had slipped off her hair and dangled around her neck. She did not seem to know or maybe she did not care. She just said, "hi," and started hop-skipping down the sidewalk.

Before I could say a word, Doris started in. "I cannot believe Mr. Kelly kept you after. On a holiday. When all you did was react. He should have kept everyone else after." Doris pressed her lips together and let a huff of air out her nose.

"I didn't remember about wearing green today until this morning at breakfast. I was the only kid in the whole dining hall with nothing green on." I pressed my hands against the backs of my arms. They sure were sore. "Noreen has a pair of green socks she wears every St. Patrick's Day. When Sharon complained she didn't have anything green, Noreen lent her one of them." I giggled. "They both look so silly with one green sock and one white one."

"But it must have saved them from a whole lot of pinching." Doris huffed again. "Whoever thought up the idea of pinching someone's arm on St. Patrick's Day because they did not wear green anyway. Besides, anyone would think a teacher would stop the kids who were pinching you instead of making the victim stay after." She carefully linked her arm with mine. "You did get out quick though."

"Mr. Kelly just wrote a sentence on the board and walked out of the room. He must have had plans to go somewhere and show off his entirely green outfit for today."

"What did he write?"

I flipped open my composition book for Doris to see. *I will not screech out in class regardless of the situation.* "Not his best sentence, but at least it's short."

"Good thing we are getting close to the end of school," Doris said. "You have only a few pages left in that thing." Doris put on a serious face. "Tell me, do you think he had on green underwear, too."

I burst out laughing, and so did Doris. We laughed all the way to the corner of Spaulding.

"See you tomorrow," Doris said between giggles.

"See you." I pressed the back of my arms until I got to The Home.

On Saturday, Patricia brought up the clean clothes for the week. My favorite dress peeked out at me from the middle of the basket. Would I be foolish to pick it this week so I could wear it on Thursday night for the concert? It hadn't brought me any luck the day of the outing. But it was the prettiest dress my size. I pulled it out and headed into the Big Girls' Room.

Patricia followed me and closed the door behind her. That reminded me of the day she'd been in the infirmary with all of us. It felt so good to know Noreen was a lot better now.

"I wanted to tell you," Patricia said. "I'm going to come to your concert on Thursday."

"You are?"

"Yes, I agreed to help walk all of the girls to school that night," Patricia said. "But I'm coming mostly to hear you sing your solo."

"Thanks." Tears surged into my eyes. It felt good to know Patricia would be in the audience.

Watching for Mom and Uncle Lloyd the next Sunday, I spied a fancy bright blue car with whitewalls and everything pulling up across the street. Did Mr. Solomon get another new car? No, I recognized Uncle Lloyd's gray fedora before I saw his face. Mom got out, and they both hurried across the street.

I opened the front door and called out, "is that your car?"

"It is now." Uncle Lloyd took the steps two at a time.

"Wow," I said. "It's a beauty."

After they signed me out, Uncle Lloyd opened the passenger door and folded the seat forward. He held his hand out like someone presenting a prize and bowed. "Welcome to my almost brand-new 1957 Chevy."

I giggled. Running my hand over the bench seat, a dazzling dark blue edged with a wide strip of light blue, I let out another, "wow!"

Mom turned in her seat. "It's a beaut, huh?"

"Uh-huh," I said. "When did you get it?"

"Yesterday." Uncle Lloyd's grin in the rear-view mirror covered his entire face.

Mom wiggled her eyebrows at me. "You should ask him why he got it."

"Okay, I'll bite," I said. "Why did you get a new car, Uncle Lloyd?"

He caught my eye in the mirror and winked. "To impress the girls."

"You mean to impress one girl," Mom said.

With a grunt, Uncle Lloyd changed the subject. "Well where are we off to today? How about the zoo?"

I held my breath.

"Sounds good to me," Mom said. "Do you like the zoo, Debbie?"

"I'd love that."

"Let's have a quick lunch," Mom said. "McDonald's sounds good to me."

"Sure thing." Uncle Lloyd started up the car. "And, let's go to the original one?"

"But, Lloyd," Mom said. "That's quite out of the way, we'll spend most of the day in the car."

"That's exactly what I was thinking." Uncle Lloyd winked at me in the mirror. "How do you feel about that Debbie?"

"Sounds like fun," I said. "This car is very comfortable."

We all laughed, and Uncle Lloyd leaned back and headed out.

We wandered around the zoo for a long time. At the bear pit, Mom grasped the railing between two of the pointy posts, and I copied her. We both studied the bear perched in a tree with no leaves and branches that had been chopped off short. To me it looked lonely.

"That bear doesn't look very happy," Mom said.

I frowned and nodded.

"That bear would probably be dead if it didn't live here," Uncle Lloyd said.

"Lloyd!" Mom swatted his arm. "What an awful thing to say."

"Well, it's true." He laughed and jerked away from Mom's swatting.

Mom linked her arm in mine nodding toward the sign up ahead. "On to the giraffes! They're my favorites."

It was past dark by the time Uncle Lloyd pulled his car up in front of The Home. I thought about inviting Mom and Uncle Lloyd to the concert, but I couldn't. What if I messed up? Or worse yet, what if missing her AA meeting made Mom mess up.

CHAPTER THIRTY-SIX

UNDAUNTED

On Thursday, after dinner, I took my time checking my favorite dress for spots and brushing my hair. Mrs. Petersen rang her little bell. "Patricia and Miss Nielsen will be walking you to and from the concert tonight," she announced. "Please be ready to leave in five minutes."

Walking along the familiar sidewalks with only the streetlights to show the way, I tried not to think about the audience filling up all those maroon velvety seats. Mary Ellen held my hand the whole way there and only let go when she saw her class lined up in the school hall.

"Break a leg," I said.

Mary Ellen jerked to a stop, her eyes big.

Laughing, I told her, "Sharon told me when you're performing that means good luck."

"Oh," Mary Ellen said. "Break a leg to you then."

Doris waved me over to get in front of her in the line following Mr. Kelly to our room at the end of the hall. I had never been in the school building after dark. Every little sound echoed. In our classroom, there was a holiday feeling with everyone standing around talking instead of sitting at our desks.

At ten minutes to seven, Mr. Kelly had the class line up in order and led us to the hall behind the auditorium. We waited outside the door to the back of the stage like we had practiced on Monday. Once all the classes were lined up, the hall was bursting with excited or nervous students. I was both. The teachers spent the whole time shushing their classes.

Mary Ellen and her class went in first with all the other first and second-graders. As they left the crowded hall, I noticed Beverly standing first in line with her class. I hardly ever saw her at school and that was fine with me. Tonight, she wore a beautiful shiny green dress, with a full skirt and a dangling bow low on her neck instead of a collar. If I hadn't known it was impossible, I would have thought she knew it was almost exactly like the one Mom wore last Sunday. She glared at me almost like she did know and was hoping I'd feel bad.

Since the seventh and eighth-grades were the last performers, Miss Bailey had told us we could leave the stage in the auditorium and find our parents there. There were two long rows of hooks for our coats in the wings of the stage. So, we all held our coats or wore them. I kept mine on, glad that Beverly couldn't see my dress.

I forgot all about Beverly when giggles and grins paraded out the stage door along with the first group including Mary Ellen's happy face. She waved and followed her classmates back to their room to wait for parents to pick them up. Miss Nielsen had already made arrangements for the girls and boys from The Home to meet near the West door. Patricia was picking up Mary Ellen from her room because she was so little.

One after the other, groups of students filed in the stage door and up the stairs to perform. After they sang, they came out to the hall and headed back to their rooms. Our group inched closer to the back-stage entrance.

When it was finally our turn, my heart was pumping like it might jump right out of my chest. We all hung our coats in the wings except for some of the boys who tossed them on the floor under the hooks.

The lights were so bright on the stage that it was impossible to see the audience. Still, I could sense their presence just like I knew I was at the Lake Michigan beach on a hot summer day even when my eyes were closed.

The audience loved "The Easter Parade" harmonies so much Miss Bailey had to stop their applause with, "Thank you, thank you, and now we would like to sing something for fun. 'It Might as Well Be Spring'."

The first notes of the song hit me like a splash of cold water. This was it. My solo.

My first line came out quieter than I meant it to. I closed my eyes, thought about the words, and sang from my heart. I sang slower like Miss Bailey taught me to letting the next words grow with feeling until the last words, "I can hope."

I lifted my chin and looked out to where the audience was listening. Miss Bailey played a bridge on the piano before an eighth-grade girl sang the next line. Each solo that followed mine was unique and fun. Jacob's solo at the end sounded wonderful. When the auditorium exploded with applause, I knew every girl and boy in seventh and eighth-grade deserved it.

I so wished Mom and Uncle Lloyd could have been there. But I knew Mom getting better was much more important. When our group sang "How Great Thou Art," it was the perfect ending. I hit every note and sang each word thanking God for all the good things in my life.

When the applause finally died out, Miss Bailey thanked everyone for coming, and we filed off the risers. Then it seemed like the whole school was on stage. Kids scurried every which way rushing to the wings to retrieve their coats and then hurrying back to find their parents. The whole time parents surged toward the stage calling out to their children.

Out of the corner of my eye, I saw Roberta heading to the backstage steps instead of going down into the audience to meet her parents. Maybe they had made arrangements to meet in the hall behind the auditorium to avoid the crowd.

Doris gave my hand a squeeze, "You were wonderful."

"Thanks, so were you," I said.

She looked out at the crowd, "There's my dad. See you after Easter." She smiled and turned to leave.

Watching her go, my heart started to thump like it had before the concert. I stood still. Patricia was probably hightailing it to the West door to supervise all the kids from The Home. It seemed like the whole city of Chicago filled up the auditorium. All those people, and, yet, not one of them was there for me. Not one person was searching the crowd looking for the student who'd sung the longest solo without one mistake.

I pulled away from all the chaos to the back of the stage to get my coat and decided to leave the way Roberta had. The West door was closer that way.

At the steps, I slowed down. Every part of me longed for a family, a family to care about how well I sang and to be proud of me. The last line of my solo rang through my mind. Gram always told me with God all things are possible.

I could hope.

CHAPTER THIRTY-SEVEN

UNTANGLE

Shoving open the door into the hall, I was surprised to find it empty. With my head full of hopes, I turned toward my classroom out of habit. Finding the door locked I laughed at my mistake. The girls' room was across the hall, and I did need to make a quick stop. The washroom at The Home was sure to have no privacy tonight.

Pushing open the door, I smelled smoke right away. I was about to back out when a voice pulled me in.

"Well look what the cat dragged in." Beverly leaned against the back wall. "Come on in and join the party."

Roberta stood in the middle of the room with her hands on her hips glaring at Beverly. She ignored me. "I'm just saying you had no right to make my sister cry. In front of her whole class."

Beverly tapped a long gold pen-like thing on the edge of the black metal trash can. A cigarette holder? With a cigarette? A ten-year-old with a cigarette? Before I could even imagine such a thing, Beverly put one arm across her chest, balanced her other elbow on her hand and waved the cigarette with its fancy holder in the air. She lifted her eyebrows and held her lips in a pout like only a highfaluting adult might do.

"It's not my fault she's such a little baby," Beverly said. "I only told her what I saw."

"You're a liar," Roberta screamed. "My father was not in his car with a strange woman."

"But I saw him. He has a green Buick, right?" Beverly tapped the cigarette holder on the edge of the trash can like that proved it.

Roberta glared at her.

"He was parked in that lot right behind the statue of von Humboldt," Beverly said as if she was describing how lovely the snow is at the park. "Maybe it was your mother. Does she have red hair?"

"Why would you tell my little sister a lie like that right before she was supposed to sing?"

Roberta's lip trembled a tiny bit. I hoped Beverly didn't notice.

"You always act like your family is perfect," Beverly said. "And, we had to stand in that line a long time. I was bored. Exactly like I am now." She tapped her cigarette holder harder, and the cigarette fell into the trash can. Then she pushed the holder together making it shorter than a pen. "I do so hate to be bored," she said. With that she swept herself out the door in her royal style.

When the door swished shut, Roberta crumpled onto the floor into a crying heap.

Without taking a moment to think it through, I tossed my coat across a sink and knelt down by Roberta. I put my arms around her. She laid her head on my shoulder and sobbed. I patted her back and said, "I'm so sorry. So sorry."

After a bit she pulled back. "Debbie?"

"I guess I came in here at a bad time," I said.

"I wish you hadn't heard that."

"Don't you worry; no one will hear any of it from me," I said. "I know all about keeping things private."

I watched Roberta's face. In only moments, it went from surprise to concern to just plain sad. Putting her head in her hands, she heaved a great sigh. "It's all an awful mess. What am I going to do?"

I got up and pulled a long strip of brown paper toweling off the roller. Getting it wet at a sink, I handed it to Roberta.

"First," I said. "You're going to get cleaned up, and I need to use the facilities." I closed a stall door and hurried to finish up. Washing my hands, I went on as if there hadn't been a break. "Then, you're going to find your parents, and I'm going to find the others from The Home. And we are both going to act like nothing happened. If anyone asks where we were, we'll just say. . . " I paused trying to think up a good lie. But I wasn't very good at it.

"We could say you fell, and I helped you." Roberta got up and went to the other sink. "But only because if we say I fell, my mother will check every inch of me for injuries. And, I thought at The Home no one would—" She stopped herself.

"You're right. No one will be checking me," I said. "So, that's a good idea. And we'd better hurry."

Roberta dried her face. "What's that smell?"

How had I missed it?

A snake of smoke rose out of the trash can, looking almost like the glittery air in the path of Mr. Kelly's projector light. I stared at it confused watching it turn thick and black and angry. Tiny tongues of flames licked the edges of the metal can. Gram's voice filled my head, *No matter what happens in your life, the Lord is always with you.*

A fire? *Please help me Jesus.*

Roberta threw the wet toweling into the fire. The can swallowed it up in a smoky gulp. "We're going to burn like those kids at that

Catholic school," Roberta wailed. Her hair swung dangerously close to the can.

"Watch out," I yelled. "Keep your hair away."

Roberta jerked back.

Cupping my hands under the faucet, I threw handfuls of water at the trash can. Most of it ended up on the floor. I kicked the can closer to the sink. The tongues of fire grew into long fingers pointing right at me. I tried to splash water from the faucet to the can. Roberta did, too. But, only drops of water reached it causing a sizzle and more smoke. I pulled off my shoe to get more water. It wasn't any use.

My coat lay across the other sink right where I put it before I hugged Roberta. That seemed like hours and hours ago. Snatching up my coat, I opened it wide, and stuffed it into the can. I could smell the beautiful blue lining burning. I stuffed harder, glad it was so thick. In barely a moment, I knew the fire was out.

Silent tears rolled down my face.

CHAPTER THIRTY-EIGHT

UNWISE

Roberta put her arms around me. "You did it," she said. "The fire's out."

"But, my new coat . . ."

Roberta got a piece of brown toweling wet and handed it to me.

"Thanks," I said wiping my face.

"And your coat," Roberta said pulling it out of the trash can. She shook it. Burnt pieces of the lining floated to the floor like ugly, black snowflakes. She brushed at it and pulled off dangling pieces. "It looks like only the lining burned," she said. A few more shakes and brushes with her hands, and she held it up for me. "Try it on. No one will see the lining."

My coat felt warm. But it smelled like smoke.

Roberta pushed the pretty wooden buttons into their unharmed loops. "It still looks beautiful. Only the lining got burned."

"Thank you," I said. She'd called my coat beautiful. It was still beautiful on the outside but being beautiful on the inside is so much more important. That's what Gram always said.

In the hallway everyone was already in line waiting for me. Miss Nielsen scowled and began leading the girls and boys out the door and down the steps toward The Home.

Outside the wind blew furiously. I hoped it blew the smoke smell away from me and my coat.

Patricia put her arm around my shoulders. "You were amazing!" She sniffed and frowned a bit.

All the way back to The Home, Patricia went on and on praising me, but her words drifted into the night air, and the wind swept them away unheard. My thoughts whirled in such a muddle that I couldn't think straight let alone enjoy Patricia's words.

We turned the corner onto Evergreen at the exact same moment Mr. Solomon's Buick whizzed by and screeched to a stop in front of their house. Roberta burst out the back door of the car and ran toward their front door.

Our whole line stopped and stared.

Her mother caught up with her and grabbed her shoulder. "Roberta, please," she shouted.

"Daddy's got a girlfriend," Roberta shouted back. "Don't you even care?"

"I'm sure you misunderstood." Her mother swept Roberta's hair behind her shoulder.

"I told you that girl saw them," Roberta shouted louder. "He didn't even deny it. What was there to misunderstand?"

"Roberta, please," her mother said again. "What will people think?"

"That's all you care about," Roberta said. "Isn't it?"

Mr. Solomon got out of the car and stood in the street. "We told you, Roberta. You misunderstood," he yelled. "And, I don't want to hear another word about it."

Roberta pushed her mother away and stood glaring at both of them.

From across the street, I could see her trembling. Without thinking, without even looking for cars, I bolted across the street. I stood next to Roberta. "It's true, Mrs. Solomon," I said. I was afraid to talk to Mr. Solomon but knew he heard me, too.

"This is none of your business, young lady." Mr. Solomon scared me spitless, but that didn't stop me.

"I was there. I heard what Beverly said she saw. She knew exactly where they were parked. She said the woman had red hair." I looked right at Mrs. Solomon's mousy brown hair.

"Get yourself back to that . . . that orphanage." Mr. Solomon pointed at The Home. "And stay out of our business."

Putting my hand on Roberta's shoulder, I stood as straight and tall as I could looking him right in the eye.

"Don't bother, Debbie," Roberta said tears streaming down her face. "They don't care." She ran up the steps and yanked the stained-glass door open. Stepping inside the house she turned and using both hands slammed the door shut shattering the glass.

An explosion of red and blue flowers blasting all over the porch.

Then Patricia had her arm around my shoulders again leading me back across the street. We walked past the line of boys and girls gawking at me, but I didn't look at a single one of them, not even Mary Ellen.

Patricia guided me all the way to my bed in the Big Girls' Room. She pulled off my shoes and socks.

Noreen and Sharon didn't say a word.

Patricia pulled off my coat. She gasped. Without asking one question she said, "I'll take this and see if I can air it out."

Patricia helped me get into my pajamas. A part of me remembered this was the same way Sharon and I had helped Noreen. Another part of me wondered why Patricia was here. The scene with Roberta was awful, but nothing like what had happened to Noreen. Why would Patricia care about me so much? I shivered as she pulled the covers up to my chin.

"I'm sorry, Debbie," Patricia said. "But there's nothing we can do. It's a private thing for their family."

Patricia left. I listened to Sharon and Noreen getting into bed. It didn't take long for Sharon's snoring to fill the quiet. Along with the whisper of Noreen's fingers on her rosary.

I made up my mind to think of anything except what had happened. But I couldn't stop thinking about my beautiful coat. It was still beautiful on the outside but so ugly on the inside.

Was that like Roberta?

I used to think so.

But, now, I wondered.

CHAPTER THIRTY-NINE

UNREAL

A shaft of sunlight swept across the night table between my bed and Noreen's. Mrs. Petersen's music drifted beneath the door. I peeked under my lashes at Sharon getting her shoes on. Noreen brushed her hair. With a glance at my bed and a nod at each other, they left the Big Girls' Room. I jumped up, got ready quick as a cricket and caught up to the line for breakfast at the bottom of the stairs.

Both Noreen and Sharon told me with their eyes they were glad to see me.

Patricia stopped at our table and whispered, "Your Uncle Lloyd called. They're coming to pick you up for lunch since it's Good Friday. When the other girls come to the dining hall, Miss Ritz said you should wait by the front door."

"Thanks," I said.

A few hours later, I stood at the front door wearing my blue coat. Two workmen were covering up the Solomon's front door with boards. It seemed like a metaphor for what I expected was going on inside the house. I could feel the crisp edges of the burnt lining in my coat. Was that a metaphor, too?

Thanks to Patricia, my coat didn't smell like smoke. I pulled my "sister" mittens from my pocket. Putting them on made me smile thinking of Mary Ellen's silly hop-skipping.

Soon enough, Uncle Lloyd's fancy new car came down the street. I did my best to act normal, but, when I glanced at Mom on the way to the car, she gave me a look. Her eyes said what's wrong? But she kept quiet while I climbed into the back.

A package, wrapped in the same paper Mom had used for my coat, sat on the seat next to me. But, today wasn't my birthday.

Mom laughed. "Got you," she said. "I know today isn't your birthday. But, it is your Gram's birthday and . . . " Mom's eyes filled up. "She would not want us to be sad. We decided she would like it if you got a gift."

Uncle Lloyd stopped and cleared his throat. "To make today a celebration that Mom's in heaven."

"Thank you." I tried to sound happier than I felt. It was such a nice idea I didn't want to ruin it. But, if Mom knew what I did to my coat, would she have brought another gift?

"Aren't you going to open it?" Uncle Lloyd said.

"Sure." Under the paper I found a box with a picture on top. Buster Brown and his dog Tige. Inside, under a layer of tissue, shiny brown Mary Janes sat waiting just for me.

"The strap can go over your foot or you can push it back behind the heel," Mom said from the front seat.

"Can I try them on?"

"Of course," Mom said. "I hope they fit."

I pulled off my scuffed oxfords. My socks looked so old. But who would notice my socks in these wonderful shoes? Picking up a shoe, I discovered three pairs of snowy-white anklets in the box, too. Tears rushed to my eyes. Mom thought of everything. Opening my eyes wide to keep the tears in, I gave her a silent thank you smile.

"They look like the right size. But, the man at the store wanted us to come back to make sure they fit properly," Mom said as if I wasn't ready to cry at all.

"Should we go there first?" Uncle Lloyd asked.

After a few swallows, I managed to say, "Yes, please. Then I can wear them to lunch."

It turned out Mom had picked exactly the right size. Uncle Lloyd insisted I choose a Buster Brown comic book as a present from him. We walked down the block from the shoe store to Wimpy's. I kept looking at my shoes so different from my old ones. I could not believe they were mine. But, mostly, I kept trying to figure out how to admit to Mom what I'd done to my coat.

"I thought that comic book would cheer Debbie right up," Uncle Lloyd said to Mom as if I wasn't walking right in between them.

"I know a secret that might do the trick," Mom said. "I'll bet she's an ace at keeping secrets."

I knew how to keep secrets better than either one of them could imagine. But I wasn't happy about it. I kept my eyes on my shoes.

"Uncle Lloyd has a girlfriend," Mom said in a silly sing-song voice.

"Really?"

"Uncle Lloyd has a girlfriend," Mom sang again.

"What's her name?" I asked. "I won't tell a soul."

"It's Patricia." Uncle Lloyd's ears turned bright red.

"I like that name," I said. "There's a worker at the Home who is always really nice to me. Her name is Patricia."

Before I could start thinking about all the things Patricia did for me just last night, Uncle Lloyd grinned. "That's my Patricia."

Then, in a big hurry, he opened the door to Wimpy's, the most hip hamburger joint in Chicago according to Sharon. He made a big fuss finding the right table and helping Mom with her coat. When he reached for mine, I said, "I think I'll keep mine on."

When he sat down, I pressed my finger and thumb together and zipped my mouth shut. Then I threw away the pretend key.

Wimpy's did have delicious hamburgers just like Sharon said, and all of us loved the French fries, too.

"Your uncle has been fixing up Gram's house, making an upstairs apartment for himself." Mom dipped a fry in ketchup, as if no one at our table had a secret at all. "You and I will have the whole downstairs to ourselves when you come home."

Home? Could it be true? I wanted to ask when, but would they still want me when they found out what I did to my coat?

"It's going to take some time," Uncle Lloyd said. "But I have a meeting with The Home's board of directors and Miss Ritz next week. We all want to be certain everything is ready for your transition. To make sure it's permanent."

"Really?" The word exploded out of my mouth. Other people in the restaurant turned to stare at us. Could it be true? Would it really happen? I hoped so. And, I would pray about it every day. Maybe Noreen would pray for me, too.

I was so happy, I didn't realize I was tapping my shoes on the tile floor until I heard the best tappy noise ever. Looking at my feet, I gave a few extra taps. How will I ever keep my feet still all day at school?

That's when I thought of Mary Ellen. I didn't want to ruin our happy time, but how could I leave her at The Home. For sure I'd have to pray about that. I just knew God could make something good happen for Mary Ellen, too.

I also knew I needed to tell Mom about the concert. But, how? I didn't want to hurt her feelings. Deciding to blurt it out, I said, "Last night at school we had a concert."

"How nice," Mom said.

I picked up my last French fry. "Actually, you might not think I'm nice at all."

"Whatever do you mean?" Mom asked.

"Could we talk in the car?"

When Uncle Lloyd opened the car door, I pulled the seat forward myself and got in the back. Both Mom and Uncle Lloyd got in quickly and turned to face me from the front seat.

"I kept wanting to tell you," I said in a rush. "I really, really, really don't want to hurt your feelings, but I was afraid I'd mess up and make mistakes, and you might think I can never do things right, and I didn't want you to miss your meeting so I never did tell you about it or invite you to hear me sing because I was afraid to."

"Oh, Debbie," Mom said. "You never have to be afraid to tell me anything."

"I'm starting to know that, but I didn't before."

"It's okay," Mom said but I could see the sadness in her eyes. "You can tell me now."

"But, it's too late now," I said. Tears came rushing down my cheeks before I could stop them. Thinking of the concert brought back all that had happened last night.

Uncle Lloyd handed me his handkerchief and turned to the front. Maybe to give Mom and me some privacy. As quickly as I could so I wouldn't chicken out, I told Mom everything including how the fire got started.

"That Beverly sounds like a terrible little girl," Mom said her voice harsher than usual. "What would ever make her pull a stunt like that? I mean, smoking? How old is she?"

"She's ten. But she acts like she thinks she's an adult."

"I suppose since so many adults do smoke, she thinks it makes her seem like one of them."

"That part wasn't a huge surprise. It's what happened after she left." I took in a shaky breath. "I still can't believe it really happened," I said. "I mean the fire."

"Oh, Debbie," Mom said. Somehow, she managed to scramble into the back seat. Putting her arms around me she held me tight. "My sweet, wonderful girl. You were amazingly clever to put out a fire like that." I could hear the tears in her voice. After Mom hugged me and shushed me and wiped my face, she said. "Lloyd, we need to go to Field's."

So, off we went. All of us shopping for another coat so Mom could take my beautiful blue one to be fixed. Mom bought me a short jacket with a zipper and a belt only in the back. It was light blue. It seemed like I was getting just as spoiled as Beverly.

When they dropped me off, Mom held both my hands and told me she loved me, and she understood. "You are the bravest girl I've ever known," she said and then kissed my cheek.

As soon as I got back to the Big Girls' Room, I spilled everything to Noreen and Sharon. Beverly, the fire, my coat, and even Mom's plans. Everything except the part about Patricia. It seemed like the right thing to do. And, it was. My roommates are the best.

Easter Sunday at the home was like pretty much every other holiday at The Home, nothing special. Lots of us went out and had fun
and food and jelly beans including Noreen and Paul who spent the
day with the Sullivans.

The rest of Easter vacation flew by, what with reading and playing
in the game room and going out to the play yard every day. On the last
day before school started again, Paul got in the boys' line to church
right across the sidewalk from me.

"Are you okay?" he asked. "Noreen told me."

"I'm fine. Tomorrow at school, I expect Beverly will pretend like
nothing happened and ignore me, like usual. But I am wondering how
Roberta is going to act."

"I want you to know, if I could, I'd go to school with you to make
sure everyone treats you right," Paul said. "Every girl ought to have a
big brother looking out for her."

My insides felt as warm as one of my "sister" mittens.

"And, I really hope things work out," Paul said. "With your family
and all."

Family? He thought I had a family? Mom and Uncle Lloyd?

Strange.

Having a family was all I could think about before the washroom
fire, only a week ago. Now, it seemed like such a long time ago. A lot
of things had changed since then.

Mostly me.

CHAPTER FORTY

UNABLE

All the way to school on Monday, I kept my eyes on Mary Ellen hop-skipping down the sidewalk. Spotting Doris up ahead leaning against our Maple, I waved. Before I got all the way there, Doris took charge of the conversation.

"I love your new shoes," Doris said. "I haven't talked to you in such a long time. Most of my Easter vacation was boring. On Easter Sunday, my dad and I went to his Navy buddy's house." She sighed. "The only other kids were two nine-year-old boys. I was supposed to keep an eye on them, but they kept hiding. The dads were all Navy guys who were on an aircraft carrier together during Korea. All they talked about was the war. One guy's wife kept crying because her brother di—um, I mean, didn't come back from Korea."

I swallowed hard and said, "That happened to a lot of families."

"I'm sorry, Debbie, I didn't mean . . . I wasn't thinking."

But tears didn't surge to my eyes, and my stomach felt normal. Now that I was getting to know Mom all over again, it wasn't so hard to think of the war and Daddy. Besides, Doris was a good friend. "It's okay, bad things happen to just about everyone."

For a moment Doris gazed down the street. I figured she was probably thinking of how her mother was sick for such a long time before she passed away. "You're right," she said. "But good things happen, too. Like your shoes."

The bell rang.

"I have lots to tell you, too," I whispered as we got in line. At the same time, I made a decision. Everything that happened after the concert was nobody's business, not even Doris'. I'd keep all that to myself and those who'd survived it.

"What happened?"

"My mom and my uncle came to visit three times." I couldn't keep the grin off my face for anything.

Doris squealed, as quietly as possible of course. "That's how you got those cute shoes. I want to hear all about it on the way home."

No surprise, that afternoon Mr. Kelly managed to dig up another World War II film. I hadn't seen the goose-steppers in so long a laugh slipped out all on its own. Why were they in almost every one of those films? Mr. Kelly glared at me, and I knew I'd have to stay after school again, so I stopped paying attention and went on a thinking trip.

Ever since I knew I would be going back to Gram's house pretty soon, I'd been worrying about Mary Ellen. Even more than I worried about leaving her behind with a new family. I tried to do what Gram said. Pray about everything and trust, but the worry kept sneaking back into my head.

And, my heart.

When Mr. Kelly had been ruining the film by telling us every detail before it started, he'd said, "Returning from the war was hard for our soldiers. They had changed from all they experienced. For some of them, the homes they'd left had changed, too." Hearing that got me to thinking. I'd changed since Uncle Lloyd brought me to The Home, and so had Gram's house. Mom had said she was in Gram's room now, and I would have the bedroom we'd shared all to myself.

I pictured that room with the yellow chenille bedspreads on the twin beds. Two beds. For only one girl. A light bulb must have appeared over my head. Mary Ellen should be in the other bed. How in the world could I ever make that happen? Somehow, I was just sure I'd figure it out.

Gram's voice filled my head, "With God nothing is impossible." Gram was right. I started praying right then. When I got back to The Home, I'd ask Noreen to get out her rosary, and maybe I could get Sharon to pray, too.

After everyone else was dismissed, Mr. Kelly assigned me an extra-long sentence, "I will not laugh at the sacrifices made by our American soldiers or tap my feet when a film is being shown."

Then he dismissed me way sooner than usual. Mr. Kelly must have had something he wanted to do again. So, lucky for me, Doris and Mary Ellen were waiting at our Maple.

"Now, tell me all about your mom and everything," Doris said putting her arm through mine as she strolled us both toward Spaulding.

All the way to the corner, I told Doris about getting my shoes as a Gram birthday present and about Uncle Lloyd building an apartment at Gram's. And how it looked like I'd be going home to Gram's house soon. I thought about that empty bed, but I didn't say anything.

"When I told Mom we had a concert," I said. "She was so sorry she'd missed it that she insisted that I sing my solo for both of them. Right there in the car."

"I bet she loved it," Doris said.

"She said I was right on key, and that I sang with so much emotion in each word, it was perfect. That's what she said anyway," I said not wanting to sound prideful.

"You sang like that at the concert, too."

"Uncle Lloyd said I sounded exactly like my mom."

"Is all of that okay?" Doris asked. "I mean, I know it must be hard. It's such a big change and all."

My throat got tight knowing how much Doris cared for me. "It feels really good being with Mom, and my uncle is so much fun. It will be nice. Really nice."

"Then I think it's all terrific."

I glanced at Mary Ellen. She was almost a half block ahead of us. I slowed down. "There's one thing though."

"What?"

"I feel dreadful leaving Mary Ellen behind."

"That is awful, but I can lookout for her at school" Doris said. "Maybe we can walk together."

"That would be nice," I said. We were almost standing still now. "Since Uncle Lloyd built the apartment, the room I'll have has twin beds."

"Twin beds!" Doris stopped. "We have to figure a way for Mary Ellen to be in one of them."

"That's exactly what I think."

"It's such a shame to waste a twin bed," Doris said. "Maybe you could sneak Mary Ellen to your Gram's house and get her to lie down on that bed and then bring your mom in the room and show her how perfect it is."

Mary Ellen had reached the corner and turned around.

"I don't know how I'd do that. But, it's a great first idea," I said. "Let's both keep trying to figure it out and talk tomorrow."

"Okay, it's a deal. I have to run."

As Doris took off, Mary Ellen tugged on my sleeve. "I gotta go."

"Then hurry," I said. "I'll catch up with you."

Mary Ellen looked both ways and crossed the street. While she ran down Evergreen toward The Home, Doris walked backward calling out "goodbye" and "see you tomorrow."

I waved longer than I needed to praying that God would help us come up with an idea to get Mary Ellen into that twin bed. When I turned around, Roberta stood in the middle of the sidewalk. I braced myself.

"Hi, Debbie," Roberta said. "I was hoping I'd see you. I know you walk home with Doris every day, but I thought, maybe, we could walk *to* school together."

Shocked, I didn't know what to say. Mr. Solomon always drove Roberta to and from school. "It is two-and-a-half blocks," I blurted out. That's not what I would have said if I'd taken the time to think. It was just in my head and out it came.

"That's okay," Roberta said. "Anyone can walk that far."

"I need to hurry today," I said. "I'm a little bit late."

"I can walk fast."

For the few minutes of our walk, Roberta chatted as if nothing awful had happened to her. And, as if we'd been great friends for a long time. I returned the favor and nodded or smiled at everything she said. But, the whole time, my mind was on my impossible prayer.

In front of The Home, Roberta crossed the street right in the middle of the block. "See you in the morning," she called.

Doris would be in for a real surprise when I showed up at our Maple with Roberta tomorrow. I think we'll both find out she's a lot more interesting than we'd thought.

Across the street I could see the front door of the Solomon's house still boarded up. Clearly, Roberta's family wasn't so perfect after all. Even though Roberta didn't mention her mother or her father, I knew in spite of how they were making Roberta pretend everything was okay, they were still a family. A family with some serious flaws, but still a family.

Maybe there weren't any perfect families.

Maybe Paul was right.

I did have a family.

And, it looked like that just might be the best family for me.

CHAPTER FORTY-ONE

WANTED

Jiggling the door knob, I opened the girls' door and dashed up to the washroom. Mary Ellen sat perched on the toilet closest to the door. I took a seat at the other end of the row. We hopped off at the same time and grinned at each other. She turned on the water at my sink and I turned on hers.

The door swung open. So much for privacy.

Mrs. Petersen filled the doorway. "Oh good, you're both here," she said. "Miss Ritz would like to see the two of you in her office."

"Both of us?" I asked. "Why?"

"It's not for me to say." Mrs. Petersen crossed her ample arms over her bosom. "Besides, I don't know the details."

I took Mary Ellen's hand, and we hurried down the aisle in the dormitory. My heart pounded so loudly I was surprised not one girl looked up. All the way down the stairs I wished I'd stopped in the Big Girls' Room to see if Noreen had her rosary out. If I knew she was praying for me, the trip to Miss Ritz' office would not seem so scary.

"Hello, girls," Miss Ritz said when we finally got there. She glanced at her wrist watch. "Please take a seat." She closed the door and went back to her desk.

We sat in the chairs against the wall. Mary Ellen did not let go of my hand. I wondered who would be filling up the two chairs in front of Miss Ritz's desk. Did Eileen have some complaint about me? Would Mr. Kelly come here to tell Miss Ritz I'd had all the sentences to write? What about Mary Ellen? Why was she here, too?

It seemed like forever, but finally someone knocked on the door. Miss Ritz got up to open it.

Mom walked in, Uncle Lloyd behind her with his hat in his hands. Smiling. Uncle Lloyd turned one of the chairs sideways toward us and took a seat.

Mom did the same with the other one smiling too, but there was something sad in her eyes.

Uncle Lloyd held out his hand to Mary Ellen. "I'm Debbie's Uncle Lloyd, and this is her mom. She's my sister." Uncle Lloyd used his thumb and one finger to shake Mary Ellen's little hand with his big one and added, "Her name is Carol."

Mary Ellen smiled, but didn't say anything. Uncle Lloyd gave Mom a confused look.

Miss Ritz went to stand behind her desk. "Let's not keep these girls in suspense. Today, the board of directors had a final meeting concerning you, Debbie. We have decided that as long as all goes well . . . "

The look Miss Ritz gave Mom when she said "as long as all goes well" made my thoughts and words get tangled into a hard ball in my throat.

Then Miss Ritz smiled at Mom. "Then the day after school is dismissed for the summer, Debbie, you will be moving back home to live with your mother."

My mouth dropped open and tears rushed to my eyes. Mom jumped up and hugged me. I would have jumped up too, but Mary

Ellen's grip on my hand kept me in my seat. I didn't know what to feel or think.

I was so happy.

But I couldn't leave Mary Ellen behind.

Miss Ritz walked over and put her hand on my shoulder. "Debbie, listen to me."

I looked up at her.

"There's more," Miss Ritz said. "After meeting your Uncle Lloyd, the board member who was contacted when Mary Ellen's father passed last August, asked me to look at this picture in her file." She handed the picture to Uncle Lloyd and looked at Mary Ellen. "He also had some very interesting questions for your Uncle Lloyd."

Uncle Lloyd knelt in front of Mary Ellen. "Have you ever seen this picture?"

Mary Ellen nodded. "My daddy showed it to me when he was sick. He said the lady in the middle was my mommy," Mary Ellen said.

"Your mommy was a very pretty lady. You look exactly like her," Uncle Lloyd said. "Then what happened."

"When I asked Daddy who the other people were, he hugged me so tight." Mary Ellen bit her lip and looked down.

"Then what," Uncle Lloyd asked.

"Daddy said, 'I'm sorry, I'm sorry.' Again and again." Mary Ellen's whole face crumpled up, and she started to cry.

I pulled her onto my lap.

Uncle Lloyd wrapped his arms around both of us.

Mom's chair fell over when she jumped up and threw her arms around all of us. I couldn't help it, I started crying too, and I didn't know why except that Mary Ellen was crying, and I knew I could never,

never, never leave her at the home. I'd have to stay too and that made me cry more. Because Mom was crying with her arms all around us and I felt my shoulder getting damp from Uncle Lloyd.

Finally, Mom got up and rummaged through her purse until she pulled out a hanky. Miss Ritz handed hankies to me and Mary Ellen. Uncle Lloyd pulled one out of his pocket and blew his nose so loudly Mary Ellen giggled, and I had to smile. She's one amazing little girl.

"Do you want to tell us the rest of the story now?" Uncle Lloyd asked.

Mary Ellen nodded. She took a deep breath that was not as shaky as her last one. "Daddy cried, too," she said. "And the nurse made me leave. I . . . I never got to ask him again." She took another shakier breath, and I thought she might start crying all over again.

Uncle Lloyd cupped her cheek and kissed the top of her head. He pointed to the picture. "Do you recognize the man?" Then he put on his hat and smiled his "say cheese" smile.

Mary Ellen looked at Uncle Lloyd and then studied the picture. "I think it's you," she said as if she liked this guessing game. "And that one's you." She pointed at Mom. "But, who's the other one?"

I leaned over to look. Gram's face smiled right at me.

"Did you know my mommy?"

"We did," Uncle Lloyd said.

Mary Ellen's lip trembled. "She died when I was born."

"We know," Mom said. "She was our sister."

"And, that means," Uncle Lloyd actually shouted. "Debbie and you, Mary Ellen, are going to come to live with us!"

"We have two empty twin beds," Mom said. "We might as well fill them both up."

My thoughts were as scrambled as a plate of eggs. Mom knew both twin beds should be filled? Uncle Lloyd knew Mary Ellen's mom? Mom knew Mary Ellen's mom? Because they were sisters? I jumped up. "Mary Ellen!" I shouted. "Do you know what that means?"

Mary Ellen gave me a confused smile.

"We're cousins!"

I pulled Mary Ellen off her chair and hugged and danced her in a circle shouting, "You're my cousin! You're coming home with me! You're going to use the other twin bed!"

Mary Ellen stopped abruptly and with a serious face said, "Can I ask you some things?" She looked at Mom and then Uncle Lloyd.

"Of course, dear," Mom said.

"Do you let girls have their own dolls?"

I heard Miss Ritz gasp.

"Yes, dear." Mom smiled, and it looked like she was holding back a laugh.

Mary Ellen glanced at me and asked, "Will Debbie have to eat squash?"

Mom looked up at me, so I gave her my squash-is-so-icky face.

"No, dear she will not."

"Just one more," Mary Ellen said. "How long until school is out for the summer?"

Laughing, Mom pulled Mary Ellen into a hug, and we all joined in. I think I heard Miss Ritz, too.

God had truly answered my impossible prayer.

The End

Acknowledgments

Thank you to: my best friend Jesus Christ; my husband Rick, who is my best friend on earth for listening to my many rambling thoughts on plot and characters, for taking me to Evergreen Street in Chicago and for knowing when to make himself a sandwich when I'm lost in the world of words; my children Michael, Jonathan, Leanne, Sherilyn, Ritch, Terianne, Jeff and their better-halves Catherine, Greg, Don, Laura, and Frank for patiently listening to me go on and on about this book; all my grands for constantly continuing to inspire me; my daughters who nagged me for years to write about my own life—I'm sorry Debbie took me down another path; SCBWI-IL and SCBWI-MidSouth for the friends who share my love of words, the conferences, and the workshops where I learned so much; and now to SCBWI-North Texas where friends are waiting to be found; Carmela Martino for the classes she taught, patiently answering so many questions; all my critique partners, for the innumerable insightful honest critiques along with their friendship, I could not have done this without you: The SWLs- Fran Sammis, Mary Jane Biscupic, Carmela Martino, Leanne Pankuch, Jill Westberg McNamara, The Ma'amuscripts- Mary Jane Biscupic, Eileen Meyer, Patti Karatotwitz, Fernanda Valentino, Cathy Velasco, Dana Easley, Julie Phend and BJ Marshall; to Word Weavers International and my WW critique partners, Tom Toya, Nicole Devries, Susan Dekins, and Jarmilla Del Boccio who also introduced me to Ambassador International; Cindy

Obenland and Nancy Manypenny my beta readers; Lt. Scott Miller (ret.) for his expertise on fires; Esther Hershenhorn who helped me find my voice; to Ron Dicerbo for taking me on as a client; Sam Lowry at Ambassador International for his email on July 12, 2018, saying he believed in me; my editor, Ashley Wallace for guiding me through the waters of "and," "so," and all my other writing quirks; Hannah Nichols for being so wonderfully creative; Anna Raats for all she did to make *Unwanted* a real book and finally to Debbie Spencer for taking over my thoughts, my fingers on the keyboard and my heart.

-FACTS-

1. **Our Lady of the Angels School,** located at 909 North Avers Avenue in the Humboldt Park area of Chicago, did have a five-alarm fire on December 1, 1958, that took the lives of 86 children and three nuns. Hundreds of lives were changed forever. The final death toll was 95.

2. **The Palmer House** was built in Chicago in 1871 making it one of the oldest hotels in the United States. It's known for its opulence and fine dining with 1,671 rooms, and it was the first US hotel to use light bulbs, a vertical steam powered elevator, and telephones. Their restaurant invented the brownie.

3. **Marshall Field's** was built in 1891-1892 in what is known as the "The Loop" area of downtown Chicago. The building takes up an entire city block from State Street to Randolph Street, to Wabash Avenue and Washington Street. The Walnut Room had a 45-foot Christmas tree annually, and the Marshall Field's Christmas window displays were viewed by thousands every year. Macy's department stores purchased Marshall Field's in 2006.

4. **Wimpy's Hamburgers** was a real restaurant chain based in Chicago that got its name from the popular Popeye cartoons created by E. C. Segar. The character named J. Wellington Wimpy loved eating hamburgers. Their signage said "Wimpy's The Glorified Hamburger."

- FICTION-

1. **The Home** is not a real place, but it is based on orphanages and homes for children in need that existed in many cities and towns in the US. Because divorce was not common in the 50s, single mothers usually depended on family and friends for the help they needed or, when necessary, made use of these institutions.

2. **Cozy Corner** in this story is an invention of my experiences and imagination. More than one independent restaurant in several states uses the name Cozy Corner.

3. **The zoo** Debbie goes to is a made-up version somewhat like both the two large wonderful zoos in Chicago and the suburbs – Lincoln Park Zoo and Brookfield Zoo.

4. **Hirsch Elementary School** is made up and all the teachers are fictitious. But it is a fact in 1958 there were no Junior-High or Middle Schools in Chicago. Debbie's school had grades kindergarten to eighth grade. And, it is also true that in the 50s some teachers made students write a sentence a hundred times expecting to improve their behavior at school.

For more information about
Mary E. Sandford
&
Unwanted
please visit:

www.mesandford.wordpress.com
www.facebook.com/MarySandfordauthor
@MaryESandford

For more information about
AMBASSADOR INTERNATIONAL
please visit:

www.ambassador-international.com
@AmbassadorIntl
www.facebook.com/AmbassadorIntl

*If you enjoyed this book, please consider leaving us a review on
Amazon, Goodreads, or our website.*